Romany in the Lanes

Phil Shelley

Illustrations

R Leonard Hollands

Lamorna Publications

Romany and Raq at the Vardo — Photograph by Peter Burton

Lamorna Publications
Yew Tree Studio, Marshwood, Dorset DT6 5QF   01297678140

First published in 2007

©Phil Shelley 2007

Illustrations © R Leonard Hollands 2007

All rights reserved

The moral rights of the author and artist have been asserted

ISBN: 978-0-9559832-0-7

Set in 11pt Verdana

Contents

		Page
Dedication		v
Foreword	Terry Waite CBE	vi
Introduction		viii
Acknowledgements		x
Chapter 1	We arrive at the Orchard	1
Chapter 2	We visit the farm and make a new friend	9
Chapter 3	We face a disaster	15
Chapter 4	The aftermath	22
Chapter 5	George and I visit the owls	30
Chapter 6	We go fishing for owls	38
Chapter 7	The Cottage	47
Chapter 8	A trip to the seaside	54
Chapter 9	The gannets, at last!	63
Chapter 10	A hard lesson in balance	71
Chapter 11	The sound and smells of the countryside	76
Chapter 12	Night time in the woods	82
Chapter 13	Stability	88
Chapter 14	The quarry	93
Chapter 15	There's more than one type of caravan	102
Chapter 16	Moving on	109

List of Photographs

	Page
Romany and Raq at the Vardo	ii
Farmer Swalwell	29
Grannie	46
Gannet	70
The Vardo today	92
George and his brother	108

This book is dedicated to Lynn, Kerry and Vicky, for all those times I wasn't there, and when the book seemed more important, at least to me.

Foreword

Terry Waite, CBE
Patron, The Romany Society
Goodwill Ambassador, World Wildlife Fund

During the many years I spent in solitary confinement as a hostage I was deprived of all communication with the outside world. For a long time I did not have access to books of any kind. As books have always been important to me this was a considerable loss. However, books are not so easily lost. When we read we form pictures in the mind. We walk through the countryside with the author and experience the warmth of the sun and the gentle touch of a summer breeze. Such pictures can stay with us long after the book itself has found its way to a second hand stall to delight another generation.

This was my experience. When I had no books at all I remembered that which I had read. I remembered rummaging through bring and buy sales in the village hall where I was able to collect many of the Romany books. They were the Wartime edition printed on economy paper, but no matter. Romany told of his visits to Cumberland in his Vardo (caravan). He had a deep affection for his dog, Raq, and made friends with the farming folk who lived and worked in those parts.

Romany died many years ago and today his name lives on through The Romany Society and of course through his books which are rapidly becoming collector's items. Phil Shelley was one of the many young people who developed their love of nature through reading the Romany books and now he has taken the story forward by writing a completely new Romany book. Phil has a fund of knowledge about Romany and the people with whom he associated. He is also a real expert on the natural world. I have walked with him in Cumberland and have envied his sharp eye which has been able to identify a bird or an animal long before I have even focused on it!

This book will hopefully introduce another generation of children to Romany, and Phil is to be congratulated on producing it. I hope that many will not only read it but will be encouraged to take a greater interest in the preservation and development of the natural world.

Terry Waite

Introduction

This book is part fact, part fiction. Although I am not 'Romany,' there was somebody who was once widely known by that name. In real life, he was the Reverend George Bramwell Evens, a minister of the Methodist Church, who was recognised in that movement for his unconventional services; services in which he spoke about the wonders of nature; of how there was a 'church' outside the obvious buildings where people worshipped; to him, that alternative church was the great outdoors.

He was born in Hull, in 1884, although living his early years in Liverpool. However, you shouldn't think of the built-up city we know today. In his time, the district in which he lived, Aigburth, was a green suburb.

At the age of thirteen, he went away to boarding school in Rhyl, and was encouraged by his headmaster to pursue his interest in wildlife. This stood him in good stead in later years when he became a famous author writing about the countryside, resulting in four books for adults and six for children. In addition, he wrote two thousand words a week for several newspapers, in his 'countryside' columns.

However, he is probably best remembered as 'Romany, of the BBC,' for he became an extremely famous and successful radio broadcaster, from 1932 until 1943, on a children's programme called 'Out with Romany,' which paved the way for modern wildlife programmes on television. People like David Attenborough and Bill Oddie owe him a debt of gratitude, because he was the first, and created the mould. He never 'talked-down' to his 13 million listeners, he involved them, and by involving them, they learned to appreciate our wonderful countryside, and all it had, and still has, to offer.

Some of the names and events I have used are real. For example, you will meet George Swalwell, a young farm boy of nine or ten years of age. He still lives close to the farm I describe in the story.

Romany's gypsy caravan was real, also. Luckily, and perhaps surprisingly, as it is made entirely of wood, it still survives, and is kept in the Romany Memorial Garden, in Wilmslow, Cheshire. His fans sent money to the BBC after his sudden death in 1943, and their subscriptions paid for the land as a lasting tribute to the man and all he stood for.

There was a thriving Romany Society until the 1960's, when it became unfashionable to be 'green.' However, enlightened fans revived the society in 1995, and details can be found on the web at www.romanysociety.org.uk.

As it says on another memorial in Cumbria, where his ashes are scattered, 'He loved birds and trees and flowers, and the wind on the heath.'

Phil Shelley, near Liverpool, August 2007

Acknowledgements

In writing this book, a long-held ambition has been achieved, so I must thank a number of people:

My wife and daughters, who have willingly accepted my enthusiasm for a man and an ideal that might make me seem eccentric to those who aren't 'in the know.'

To those friends whose names I have used in the book. Whilst this essentially a work of fiction, I hope you don't feel misrepresented. Particular thanks to the Swalwell family: George, his wife Mary and daughter Sue, who not only allowed me to weave my story around them, but provided most of the original photographs reproduced in the book.

To Ray Leonard Hollands, my talented artist friend, who produced the wonderful illustrations; I know it was a labour of love as Ray's whole life has been inspired by Romany.

Terry Waite, CBE: internationally recognised humanitarian, Patron of the Romany Society and long-time Romany fan; thanks for the great foreword.

Lastly, but extremely importantly, to Romany's surviving family: Romany Watt, his daughter, and his grandchildren, Roly, Jennie, Simon and Ben, for graciously giving me permission to write as though I were the great man himself, even though I could never equal his works.

Chapter 1

We arrive at the Orchard

The slow, rhythmic squeak of my caravan's wheels was almost hypnotic, as their iron-bound rims bit into the rough road surface.

For a long time, I had yearned to own a 'vardo,' the gypsy word for 'caravan.' Perhaps it was because my mother was a true gypsy, of the 'Smith' family. She was born in a caravan, as were her brothers and sisters, father, mother and grandparents. As far back as I could trace, my ancestors had lived the free life on the road. Their home was made wherever there was space to light a fire, water nearby, and fresh, cool grass to graze the horse. Selling wooden clothes pegs made from the very trees that shaded the vardo, gave them a living. They claimed they had the ability to tell fortunes, and many a housewife was happy to pay to hear what their future held in store.

And so, one day, with gypsy blood in my veins, and dreams in my heart, I had passed by Brough Hill Fair, near Appleby-in-Westmoreland. A gypsy encampment caught my eye, and I stopped to talk to the families. It's not wise to get straight to the point with gypsies; there are certain rules to observe.

For a while, we spoke of gypsy families that we knew well, the Lovells and Grays, and of my own family, many of whom were known to my new friends. After a while, they invited me into their vardos; a sure sign of their growing confidence in me. This meant the time was getting close when I could raise the subject of buying a caravan of my own.

Gypsy tradition dictates that a vardo is burned after the owner dies, although this was becoming less common in modern times. When the moment seemed right, I mentioned my interest in owning a vardo. Yes, they had one for sale and would I like to see it? I almost leaped from the steps in my eagerness to discover what they had to offer, but realised just in time that this would give the wrong message, and might prevent them selling it to me.

So, sedately, I wandered across to a dirty, yet brightly painted van parked away from all the others. The eldest man of the group explained that the previous owner had died and his daughter had married a 'gorgio,' (non-gypsy) so had not wanted the caravan. We talked of everything but the price, as is their way, and then eventually we settled for £75. It seemed such a lot of money to pay for a vardo, particularly one in that condition, and yet I knew that the pleasure it would give me would repay me many times. In case you are surprised at the price, I must tell you that this was the year 1921, so it really was quite a sum!

As I have said, it was painted in the traditional bright colours, which was not at all what I had in mind, but I could see beyond the grime and gaudy colour scheme. I hired a horse from one of the gypsies and drove away the proud owner of my very own vardo.

Back home, I cleaned it up and made some alterations. Then, with a coat, or two of fresh green and cream paint, I had driven it to a lonely spot, close to the

Scottish border, where it rested for almost ten years. I had moved it around the north quite a bit since then, but today, I was again on the road to find it a new home, somewhere near to Whitby, on the East coast. I had tired of the same scenery and my objective was to be in an area largely unknown to me. Who knew what adventures lay ahead, what animals and birds I might observe, what new friends I might make?

I knew exactly the type of place I was looking for; a spot close by a river, both to give me a source of clean drinking water, and to give me the chance for fishing. In addition, nearness to nature was of importance in the selection of a site. Comma, my faithful horse, (so named because she never came to a full-stop!) was becoming tired. Those hills West of Whitby had taken her by surprise. They were so steep and long, but, as always, she had tried her best, and now she was ready to make the most of the long grass at the wayside.

What a day it had been! In the hedgerow, sparkling with hawthorn blossom, I had seen a blue tit seeking out its diet of insects, a pair of goldfinches for whom spring was the beginning of a very busy period feeding their young, and a youthful stoat, whose high-spirits made him seem like a tap-dancer.

Blue Tit

He had appeared upset at our arrival, bravely chattering at Comma, who must be at least two hundred times larger than him! Raq, my cocker spaniel dog, didn't quite know what he should do. Normally he would defend the vardo, which he regards as home, but he was rather put-out by this noisy interloper, deciding that caution was the better way. We soon passed him by and left him to seek out his prey.

It was close to evening when my old vardo drew alongside an orchard in which the trees were simply bursting with pink and white blossom. There was an undertone of insect sound; the bees swayed from flower-to-flower, in their perpetual quest for nectar. I had a warm feeling about this place. It would be good to spend some time here.

"Whoa, old girl," I said, at the same time gently pulling back on the reins. I could almost feel the silence as the vardo creaked to a standstill. In the distance a wood pigeon was calling, "Take two coos, Taffy," it said.

Somewhere, out of sight, a tinkling river was singing. Now, if we could only manage to squeeze the vardo between the apple trees, and if the farmer was friendly, and if the ground wasn't too soft .... so many questions to be answered, but nobody around to ask!

My thoughts were disturbed by Raq, who was giving his soft 'stranger about' type of growl. His hearing, and, for that matter, all of his senses are so much keener than mine.

From within the trees a hidden voice said, "Looking for a campsite, are you?"

"It's getting late, and my horse is tired," I replied, all the time straining to spot the man behind the short speech.

"You could do worse than just here," he said, stepping out from behind a large tree. His appearance was exactly that of a typical farmer; worn, brown corduroy trousers, with a patch on one knee, a jacket that had definitely seen better times, and on his head a battered, chocolate-coloured trilby hat. He had a wide smile that said, 'welcome,' putting me at my ease. More importantly, I saw that Raq's stubby tail was vibrating so quickly that it could power a generator; a dog quickly recognises a friend from an enemy.

"It would just be for a few nights," I said, hesitantly.

"Stay for as long as you like. The ground is dry, even though the river's close by, and we won't be picking the apples until much later in the year," he responded. "Let me guide you in," he finished.

I stepped down from the running board of the vardo, taking Comma's reins in my left hand. She seemed disappointed at having to work again, just as she was beginning to enjoy the rest. But she responded to my gentle, "Come on, Comma, just a few more steps," and the vardo lurched its way beneath the trees.

"Take care of your chimney," the farmer warned.

On a British vardo the chimney pot is always on the right-hand side, to avoid overhanging branches as it moves down a road. On this occasion we were completely surrounded by trees, and an accident seemed almost inevitable. However, with careful and steady handling, we advanced the necessary twenty-five yards to reach the open space, without mishap.

Despite the fact that it was growing late, sunlight still entered the leafy glade. I knew from its direction on the rear-window of the vardo, that the morning sun would shine on the steps, which was exactly what I wanted. There is nothing nicer than sitting on the running board, watching the sunrise, listening to the dawn-chorus, with a freshly-brewed mug of tea in my hand.

I searched around for a few large stones to place underneath the wheels. The vardo has a loose and rather ineffective brake, so, when we stop, it's important to jam the wheels in position to prevent a nasty accident. I stamped them in place with my foot, and, satisfied that it was as safe as it was going to be, I turned to thank the farmer, to find he had disappeared as quickly as he had arrived.

"How strange," I muttered to Raq. I often find myself talking to him when I don't have human company. He just wagged his tail and carried on exploring his new home.

It was high time we ate, but by my rules, Comma always comes first after a hard day pulling a ton of vardo. I mixed her meal, and slipped on her nosebag. Her contented munching told me that she appreciated my work. And now to Raq and me!

I cast around for some dry sticks, and soon found what I needed. I made a small pile of them to one side of the vardo, but far enough away so that smoke and sparks would not be a nuisance. From one of the convenient store-boxes on the front of my wooden home, I fetched some dry wood-shavings that I always carry for fire-starting; you can't guarantee to find dry wood in the British countryside!

Placing the shavings beneath the sticks, I struck a match, and soon had a blaze going. A heavy iron pot and kettle were within reach, and the woodland clearing quickly smelled of a tasty stew in the making. The steam escaping from the kettle-spout told me it was time to make tea.

Settling down with my back against one of the large wheels that had carried me so far, I began to enjoy my meal. Raq was by my side, quickly eating his dinner. Dogs' always finish within seconds, and don't have any table manners at all. Then again, in the wild it's a case of 'first-come, first-served,' and there's no room for polite behaviour, or you will go hungry.

However, even though there was still some meat left in his bowl, Raq stopped eating and looked up. There was a snuffling sound nearby, very much like a tiny steam-train. The grass parted at the edge of the clearing, and out popped a hedgehog, or 'hotchi,' as the gypsies call them.

As I have explained, my ancestors all lived in vardos, and one or two of them were quite famous. Gypsy Smith, a travelling preacher, was my uncle. His sister, Tilly, was my mother. She was also a preacher, and was quite well known throughout the country for her 'revival meetings.' My boyhood was spent travelling around from town-to-town, city-to-city, very much the lifestyle of a modern celebrity. Suitcases were my wardrobe; other people's houses were my home. That is until we settled in Liverpool, in a house we called 'Miro Tass,' or 'My Nest,' where I lived until I was thirteen, when I went off to boarding school in Rhyl, North Wales.

However, back to our hedgehog. His eyesight is not very sharp, but he more than makes up for this with his keen sense of smell. His diet is not really one that we would enjoy; slugs, beetles and other insects are his favourites.

Raq wanted to run over to this intruder and frighten him away, but I stopped him, preferring to see what the hedgehog would do. Occasionally I could hear a 'crunch,' as he found something tasty to eat. Slowly, he made his way across the clearing, only changing his course when he smelled something good.

Either he didn't see us, or he didn't think that we were a threat, as he passed within a few feet of where we sat, as still as rocks. Raq trembled as he drew close, but he knows who is master; he stopped himself from attacking simply because I had said, 'No!'

When the hedgehog had gone, and the noise he made had faded away, I said a simple, "Kushto Juckal,' which means 'Good boy,' and his tail again became a dynamo as he finished his food.

"It's time we turned in, old man," I told him.

I took the kettle from the fire, and we went up the vardo steps into our mobile-home, where I used the remaining hot water to wash our dinner dishes. I then emptied the washing-up water over the fire to be sure that all danger from it had gone.

From inside one of the long bench-lockers that run along each wall of the vardo I took out my bedding and a set of wooden planks. The lockers were part of my handiwork when I first bought the vardo, and I am very proud of them.

While I often sleep outside in a tent, this evening I was so tired that I simply couldn't face the thirty minutes, or so, it takes to put it in place. So tonight, the vardo would become my bedroom.

I placed the ends of the planks on the rails above the lockers, dropped my mattress in place, and I had a rough, but ready, bed upon which to lie. Raq settled down beneath the bed, and from his snores I could tell that he had quickly dropped-off to sleep.

Despite my tiredness, I found sleep difficult. The sounds of the orchard drifted-in through the open vardo window: the 'kee-wick' of a tawny owl, as it called to its mate; the sharp bark of a fox somewhere in the distance; the singing of the river nearby. The sounds filled my mind and yet soothed me. To be so in touch with nature had long been my dream, and now, here I was, living out that wish.

Lazily, my thoughts drifted to the sudden arrival and equally hasty departure of the farmer; I hadn't even had time to ask his name before he had melted away into the trees. Ah well, plenty of time for that tomorrow. I would need to call at his farm for milk and eggs for my store-cupboard. It's a hungry life on the open-road!

'Tomorrow .... Tomorrow;' before I knew it, the sounds and my thoughts had become one, and I slowly drifted off into a deep sleep.

Chapter 2

We visit the farm and make a new friend

The sun was already streaming through the windows that are set into the vardo door. Inside, the caravan had become very hot and dry. Poor Raq was looking really thirsty by the time I threw off the covers and climbed down from my bed. I had been so tired last night that I'd forgotten to leave him a bowl of water. He looked at me as if to say, "Please can I have a drink?"

"I'm sorry, Raq, but you were just as weary as I was. Here, have this."

I filled his bowl from the small water tank just inside the vardo door. The water merely trickled out, telling me that I would have to get some more before I could have a wash, or even my morning tea; it was to be my first job of the day.

Fetching the bucket from the hook under the vardo, I wandered in the direction of the river-sounds that had played all night in my dreams. Within a short distance, I found what I was looking for; the River Esk!

Kneeling at the water's edge, I dipped the bucket into the fast-running river. It was almost full when I heard a bird calling that always reminds me of quick-flowing streams. "Chiss-ick, chiss-ick," it went. I looked upstream and a sudden movement on a large rock caught my eye; it was, as I expected, a grey wagtail. I always feel this is a poor name for such a lovely bird.

From its title, you would think it to be all grey in colour. Now, while it does have some grey on its back and the top of its head, it is the stunning yellow colour, starting beneath its black bib, covering its chest and on down to meet its tail, that always takes my breath away. This was a male bird, as it had a black bib – the female looks almost identical, but has no bib, only a pale throat.

Just like a ballet dancer, it is always on the move. Hardly for a moment does it stand still, bobbing and flicking its tail in a merry dance.

I was just wishing I'd brought along my binoculars when it was off! It flew straight down the river, past where I was crouching, to alight on yet another rock, and perform its little salsa all over again.

I raised the bucket, by now heavy with water, and decided that as soon as I had a chance, I would find the wagtail's nest and take some photographs. Did I mention that photographing wildlife is a hobby of mine?

Back at the vardo, it was time for breakfast. The smell and sizzling sound of bacon soon filled the clearing, and, when all was ready, I settled on the vardo steps to eat my fill. Food always tastes so much better when cooked out-of-doors, especially so on an open-fire. The smell of wood-smoke adds a flavour that says, 'these are lazy days. Rise from bed when you like, go to bed when you are tired. In between, do nothing, or do everything. You are a part of nature. Do nothing that will harm her, and, in turn, she will look after you.'

As usual, I allowed my mind to wander. The warm sun beat down, the few cotton-wool clouds drifted slowly along, and I was in no rush to get up from my comfortable seat on the vardo.

"Something smells good!"

The voice startled me; even Raq had not heard the farmer approaching, and he greeted him with a series of sharp, frightened barks. He soon settled down, however, when a biscuit was thrown in his direction.

"This is the last of my bacon. Is there somewhere nearby where I might be able to stock-up?" I asked, hoping all the while that he might suggest the farm.

To my delight he replied, "I'm sure we can spare some at Carr End," which was clearly the name of his farm. "Call in later this morning," he ended.

"I'll be along as soon as I've cleared up," I told him.

He made his way across the clearing, and was soon out of sight amongst the apple trees.

"It seems we have an appointment, Raq," not, of course, expecting a reply, but his wagging tail told me he at least agreed!

It was while I was clearing away my breakfast dishes, that I heard a loud and very distinct laughing-sound close to the vardo. "Yap-yap-yap-yap-yap." I knew instantly that it was a green-woodpecker. The old country name for this bird is 'yaffle,' which describes its call perfectly.

I looked out of the vardo door, and caught a glimpse of green, yellow and red, as it shot away into the tree-tops.

Green Woodpecker

"I bet it's nesting nearby," I thought. "If it is, I'm going to photograph it," I promised myself.

I closed the vardo door and headed-off in the direction I'd seen the farmer take. Within a short distance we joined a well-worn path, taking the direction of a distant roof-top that I took to be Carr End Farm.

Within ten minutes, Raq and I were entering a well-kept farmyard, to the sound of several barking dogs. There is no better alarm for a farmer than a dog.

Although they were securely chained, I put Raq on his lead, as he was on their territory and I didn't want to upset them.

The door of the farmhouse opened, and out stepped the farmer, whose name I still did not know. This time he had removed his jacket and was in his shirt with the sleeves rolled up.

"I wondered whether you'd find us," he said by way of greeting.

"It was easy enough when we got out of the orchard," I replied, adding, "I hope you might be able to spare some eggs, milk, butter and bacon."

"I leave that side of things to t' missus," was his response. "Mary," he called, "here's the gypsy I told you about."

The farm door opened again and out came his wife. She was a large lady, wearing a clean white apron, with flour all over her hands and face.

"You'll have to excuse me, "she began, "you see it's my day for baking."

As she spoke a delicious smell drifted from the open door.

"Rhubarb pie, if I'm not mistaken," I drooled!

"You're right, Mister..... err?"

"Call me Romany," I interrupted, "everyone does."

"It *is* rhubarb," she said, adding; "You can take one with you, if you like ... Romany."

"I'd love to, Mrs..... I'm sorry, but I don't know your name either," I laughed.

"It's Horton," the Farmer said.

"Well, now that we know each other, I'll tell you why I'm here. Mr Horton and I met earlier; I hope it's alright with you, Mrs Horton, but I wonder if you could spare some milk, eggs, butter and bacon?"

"We run a farm, Romany; we've always got plenty over," she replied, "I'll get them," and she went back into the farmhouse.

While she was gone, I spoke to the Farmer about his farm. I learned that he kept sheep, dairy cattle, for milk, and, of course, had a nice crop of apples each year from the orchard where the vardo lay.

"Would it be alright if I fished the river? Do I need a permit?" I enquired.

"I own the stretch below Sleights Bridge, down past the orchard," he told me, "and you're welcome to try your luck."

I already had a vision of grilled trout, followed by Rhubarb pie, for dinner that evening, so was pleased with his answer.

Mrs Horton emerged from the farmhouse with my groceries, for which I paid her, and then, thanking them both, I turned to leave the yard.

Just then, a commotion near the dog kennels caught my attention; two black and white dogs were nipping at a third dog, similar to them in every way, but size.

The farmer shouted at them to stop, and the two larger dogs slunk back into their kennel.

"Always a problem with the runt," he remarked, meaning the last-born. He went on, "I'm getting rid of her today; she's no use at all."

"What do you mean, 'getting rid,' Mr Horton?"

"It's down to the vet in Whitby, for her, I'm afraid. No self-respecting farmer wants her as a working dog, so I'll have to have her put down," he said. "No room on a farm for an animal that doesn't earn its keep."

I was shocked at his response, but realised that to a farmer, his business was the farm, and all unnecessary costs had to be avoided. Still, it seemed a bit harsh as she looked a pleasant little thing.

Just then she padded quietly over to me; all the while her long tail was flapping behind her. She cowered down as she got near. Raq just stood stock-still and watched, but I noticed that his tail was wagging.

"Hello girl," I whispered as I knelt to stroke her.

At this, she licked my hand in a most friendly way and my heart melted. How could I see her destroyed when my vardo had room for another little body?

"How much do you want for her?" I found myself saying.

"Do you mean you'd take her, even though she's the runt?" Farmer Horton asked.

"Often the last born makes the best pet," I told him. "They've got more to prove."

"In that case, you can have her. You'll save me a job," he said.

Not wanting to know the details of what that job might be, I quickly bundled her up, thanked him, and left the yard before he changed his mind.

I returned to the vardo and introduced my little friend to her new home. She wasted no time, bounding up the steps and finding the food cupboard right away! A sharp, "No," was all that was required and she moved away to the other side of the van.

She quickly settled down, soon falling asleep beneath one of the bench seats where I had deliberately made a gap for Raq to sleep.

"So, what do you think old man? What shall we call her?"

Working collies often have traditional names, and I wanted to stay with this pattern. Was it to be 'Mirk,' or perhaps 'Heather?'

I couldn't make up my mind, and thought I would leave the decision for now. However, with a new dog on my hands this afternoon's fishing trip wasn't going to be possible. I'd need to see how well behaved she was before I could risk taking her down to the river and leaving her on the bank. That meant I would have to raid my store cupboard, and make the most of Mrs Horton's rhubarb pie instead!

Chapter 3

We face a disaster

I spent the afternoon around the vardo. A little bird-watching followed lunch, then a game with Raq and Meg, as I'd decided to call her, who seemed to enjoy each other's company. Raq showed no sign of jealousy, and I was careful to make sure I treated him as Meg's boss. Dogs need a very clear order of importance, or they become very difficult to manage, so the new dog needed to know her place. That meant putting Raq first for everything – first with food, first through the door, first to be spoken to.

In the later afternoon the weather, which up until now had been beautiful, became unsettled. The change began with a light breeze coming from the direction of the sea. I first noticed it when the rustling of the apple trees became louder than the 'pink-pink' call of the chaffinch.

"We may be in for a storm," I said to the dogs. Both tails wagged, although I doubt that they understood.

I have spent many wet nights in the vardo, so I know exactly what needs to be done. The tent could wait for another time.

I made sure the fire was out and put my pans and buckets beneath the vardo out of the way of the rain. Down came my shirts that I had on the home-made washing line; the earlier sun had made them perfectly dry. They were stowed in the little clothes-locker, half-way down the inside of the vardo, near to the heating stove.

I then walked around the clearing collecting more dry wood; any rain would make fallen branches unusable for several days.

Finally, I was satisfied that I'd done everything I could. Let the storm come; we would be fine and dry inside the vardo.

I made a meal for the dogs, putting Meg's food into an ordinary dish. I must add 'extra dog-bowl' to my shopping list when I go into Whitby!

I thought that I might do a little writing, but despite the early hour, I found I couldn't see the paper clearly.

"Might be an idea to light the lamps," I informed the dogs.

I lifted the glass chimney from each oil-lamp, carefully adjusted the wicks, and lit them, placing the chimneys back in their holders.

The whole vardo took on a warm, golden glow, with shadows gently flickering in the far corners. I love this time of day, feeling so cosy and just thinking about my adventures; the birds, animals, insects, wild-flowers I've seen; how Raq chased that rabbit, never, of course, managing to catch it. These days we spend so little time day-dreaming it is becoming a lost art. Every day, just ten-minutes spent in a little world of our own would make us so much more relaxed.

I came back to the real world and began to write.

An hour or so must have passed, when I found myself yawning. I never watch the clock when I'm at the vardo; I go to bed when I feel tired and I get up when I awake, usually quite early.

"Time for a last look outside, you two," I told the dogs, opening the vardo door. They ran down the steps and I was shocked to see it was snowing – but in May? The wind had become stronger, and I could see the branches of the apple trees swaying and I realised that some of the blossom was being blown off the trees, looking just like snowflakes. It had also begun to rain.

"Hurry up," I shouted to the dogs, raising my voice above the sound of the wind and the rustling leaves, just to be heard. They bounded up the steps, Raq first, of course, and promptly shook themselves dry, soaking me and the vardo.

"You could have waited for the towel!" I told them rather crossly.

I got the dog-towel from a drawer and proceeded to rub them as dry as I could make them.

When I was happy that I had done all that I could, I put the towel near to the stove and put a match to the paper and twigs that were always left inside, ready to be lit if needed. Although the day had been warm, there was now a chill in the air which the heat from the oil-lamps had only partly taken away.

"Time for bed," I told the dogs. Although Meg was new to the vardo and our way of life, she couldn't have behaved any better. She followed Raq to the little sleeping area I'd made, and settled down next to him on the old bed-cover he has for his bed.

"They look really comfortable," I thought, as I made my own bed.

When it was ready, I pressed the little lever on each lamp that puts out the flame, and climbed into bed.

I never find sleep difficult, and within a few minutes had drifted off.

"Crash!"

"Woof, woof, woof!"

I almost fell out of bed with fright.

"What on earth was that?" was my first thought; "Is the vardo alright?" was my second.

I quickly lit a lamp, and dashed to the door. I opened the top half a little way, held the lamp up, and peered out. No more than twenty-five yards away there was a huge branch from an apple tree lying on the ground. However, what shocked me even more than our close shave was the fact that the branch was partly under water.

"The river must have burst its banks," I remarked to no-one in particular. "Let's hope the rain eases-off before things become dangerous."

I knew that Comma would be alright, as she would simply move to higher and drier ground.

There was nothing else I could do but go back to bed and hope the rain would stop and the river-level lower. Then the thunder began! Being in the vardo was like being inside a huge bass-drum while the drummer was beating it with a heavy drumstick.

'Boom, crack, crash,' echoed the thunder; 'Pitter, patter,' tapped the raindrops. Both were accompanied by a fireworks display created by the searing white lightning-bolts. The only thing missing from this weather-orchestra was the string section. If I wasn't so worried, it could have been almost beautiful. The complete power of nature over man was so obvious; nothing yet invented could stop this awesome concert, and I was simply a member of the audience.

Another branch tumbled to the ground, and I guessed that the tree from which it had fallen had been struck by lightning. I could only hope that any more falling branches would miss the vardo; it was all a matter of luck; I was completely helpless.

Hours passed with no obvious change to the weather; the thunder still roared overhead, and the sound of the torrential rain had become a constant buzz on the vardo roof.

Suddenly, above the din I heard a sound like paper tearing only much, much deeper and louder. There was a tumbling noise reminding me of a huge stone-fall, followed by three tremendous crashes. I could only think that some nearby building had collapsed; what if someone were trapped inside?

I rushed to the vardo door and opened it wide; quick as a flash, Meg ran past me and jumped straight off the top step of the vardo. There was a great splash as she went straight into the now deep water. It was as black as coal outside and, although I could hear her cough and splutter, I could see nothing; she was clearly in trouble.

I dashed inside to fetch the lamp, when there was another splash; where was Raq?

I hastily lit the lamp and ran back to the door. I peered outside, but could see no sign of either dog. The water, which had been several inches deep when I'd looked out earlier in the evening, was now almost up to the top of the vardo wheels and they are thirty inches high! It was moving fast, just like a river, and I was concerned that the dogs might have been swept away.

I began to remove my shirt, imagining that I would have to get into the water to search for them, when a quick, sharp bark made me run back to the door. Close to the steps was Raq, and in his mouth he had Meg's collar – slowly pulling her along as he struggled to keep afloat!

I reached out and grabbed Meg by the scruff of her neck and hauled her onto the step. Once I was sure she was safe, I stretched my arm out and found Raq's collar. Without hesitating, I pulled him towards me, but the leather of his collar was wet and slippery and the current was so strong that he slipped away. He disappeared under the water in a mass of bubbles, so I moved down onto the second step and a little way into the water. Reaching underneath at the spot where he went down, I managed to touch the top of his head, but again he slipped away. With one last effort I managed to grab his collar, but this time locking my fingers underneath. One great heave and up he came, landing on the step like a big salmon.

For some moments Raq and I lay there, panting and dripping.

After a while I said, "That was close, you two. Let's hope we don't have to swim for it later."

It was now obvious that the river had flooded, and I could only pray that the rain would stop before the vardo was completely under water.

I began to think about what we might do if that happened. I decided that the only option was to make a raft from the timbers I used for my bed. Getting some rope from under the benches, I tied the planks together as best I could, but all the time worrying that it might not hold together.

How could I keep both dogs on board a raft, and to where would I paddle? Throughout the next few hours these questions, and more, turned over and over in my mind.

It was around four o'clock in the morning when I noticed the rain had ceased.

"Let's hope that's an end to it," I said, and the dogs' tails showed they agreed.

At six o'clock it was getting light, so I looked out of a side window. The orchard looked a complete mess. There were several large boughs on the ground, and many smaller branches lay scattered like a huge spider's web.

"The farmer won't get his crop of apples this year," I thought to myself.

The really good news, though, was that the water-level was now a lot lower. I carefully opened the door a little way, not wanting a repeat of last night's dog-drama.

To my delight, I could see the top three steps leading up to the running-board. Another hour or two at this rate, and it might be safe to get out.

Over to my left, on a hillock, Comma was grazing, almost as though nothing had happened. It was just as I'd expected; when the ground became wet she'd done the clever thing, and moved higher. It was still a matter of good fortune, though, that she hadn't been struck by a falling branch.

"Just a while longer," I remarked to the dogs. "We've waited all night and a few more hours' won't hurt."

Chapter 4

The aftermath

Sure enough, by the time eight-thirty had arrived, the ground was wet, yet sufficiently firm to support my weight. After first letting the dogs out to explore, I went outside for my first proper look around since the storm.

From the window the damage to the orchard had appeared bad; now it looked complete. There wasn't a single tree that I could see on which there was any blossom left, and many had lost large branches.

I heard some squelching footsteps approaching, and was greeted with, "Just came to check you were OK," from the farmer. "That was some storm," he added.

"We're fine, thanks," I informed him, and I told him the tale of the two dogs.

He mentioned that he'd lost some sheep from his lower fields, but that the farm had missed the water completely, as it was on higher land.

"What about Sleights Bridge?" he asked me. "It'll need a full re-build," he commented.

"Is that what I heard?" I exclaimed. "I was worried it might have been a house, with people inside."

"Swept clean away," was how he described the disaster.

I decided this might be a good time to say what had been on my mind all night.

"I'm very grateful for your hospitality, Mr Horton, but after last night I'm going to move on to another spot. I can't risk another flood like that one."

"I understand," he replied. "I've never known the Esk to flood like that before, but you never can tell; it just might happen again."

"Is there anywhere you can suggest?" I enquired, hoping he might know another friendly farmer.

His reply was not what I'd hoped for: "Not really," but then, helpfully, "If I were you I'd head further down the road you were on when I saw you the other day. You'll pass several farms and on better and higher ground, too."

"While I've been here, I've seen a couple of birds I'd like to photograph. Would that be possible?" I enquired.

"Yes, of course it will. But how will you get close enough?"

"I'll set-up my hide," I told him.

"Don't get washed away then!" he laughed.

After he'd gone, I whistled for Comma and she came ambling over to me, seemingly without a care in the world.

"Sorry, old girl, but its back in the shafts for you; at least for a couple of hours."

She made no complaint as I buckled on her harness. When all was ready I slowly backed her in between the two shafts that hook onto the front of the vardo. When she was in position I then attached the shafts to her harness.

"Come along, Raq and Meg," I called, and, as good as gold, they both ran to join me at the vardo.

"We'll need to be a bit careful getting out of the trees," I informed the dogs. "There's no farmer to guide us through this time."

Very slowly we edged our way between the apple trees, taking care to avoid the fallen branches. Although the ground was very soft in places, we managed to steer away from the worst patches, and only became stuck once. But a quick push from the back of the vardo got us moving again.

We reached the road, and I breathed a sigh of relief. "That could have been a lot worse," I thought.

I sat on the running board, sweat running down my face. The dogs jumped up after me, Raq first, followed by Meg, naturally!

With a, "Come on, Comma," and a gentle flap of the reins, we were off; slowly at first, the speed then building up to a steady pace, slightly faster than a man could walk. There was no hurry, I felt confident that we would find a new site before nightfall.

Within a few minutes we came to Sleights Bridge, or what was left of it. Most of the stonework was now lying in the river and I could see that it would need many months work to repair it. Perhaps a new one would be necessary, maybe in another place. How lucky it was that it was not being used at the time.

I passed one or two farms, but they were down such steep lanes that I knew we would have trouble getting the vardo to them.

I was beginning to think we might have to camp at the side of the road when another farm appeared on our left. This time the buildings were actually on the roadside. Outside there was a large stone with the name 'Cragg Farm' chiselled into it. I pulled the vardo to a halt with a, 'Whoa, Comma."

I noticed that Raq's tail was wagging almost as strongly as a windmill in a gale. Seated on the wall, just to one side of the sign, was a young farm-boy, who was eyeing the vardo with some surprise. It's hard to remember who first broke the silence, but I recall saying "Hello. Do you think I might speak to your father, please?"

"He's in the barn," he replied, adding, "I'll fetch him."

He ran off across the yard, looking back twice as he went.

He was gone for a minute or so, and then came back into view with a man by his side. I couldn't hear what was being said, but the boy was clearly excited, as he was pointing at the vardo as they walked.

"George here tells me you'd like a word," opened the farmer.

"Yes, please."

I introduced myself, adding, "I'm sorry to take you away from your work, but I'm looking for somewhere to park my caravan."

I explained what had happened the previous night, adding, "We're all a bit tired, as you can imagine."

"I do have a field that I don't plough," he informed me. "You can't get to it from here with that, though," he remarked, pointing at the vardo. "It's far too steep down through the yard and beyond. You'll have to go up the lane to the second gate, and then we can help you down from there."

"That's very kind, "I said. "Would you like to jump on board?" I asked the boy.

Without hesitating he was up and sitting next to me before I knew it!

"Let's go, Comma," I called, and we were away.

"I see your name's George," I mentioned.

"Yes, George Swalwell," he responded. "Slow down now," he said, "the gate's just around the bend."

"Wait here," he told me, and he jumped off the vardo.

He ran to the gate, undid the fastening, and opened it wide. While he held it back, I gently steered Comma and the vardo between the large stone gate-posts. There was plenty of room to spare as it was obviously built to take farm-carts.

Across the fields, from the direction of the farm, I could see three men and another boy approaching.

"It's my Dad and a couple of the workers," George kindly said. "My brother, Wilf, has come to help, too."

We waited for them to reach us, and then the dogs jumped down, giving them a yapping, but friendly welcome.

"You'll need a hand to get down the slope, even from here," said Mr Swalwell. "We'll stay at the front end, and hold the van off your horse. It looks as though it will be too heavy for her on her own."

"I'll put a rope around the back axle, that way I can also take some of the weight. Do you think you can steer her, George?"

"Of course I can," he said eagerly, taking the reins from me and climbing up on the running board.

I went into the back of the vardo and brought out a length of strong rope. I passed it over and around the rear axle, tying a knot to form one long loop.

"Ready," I called. "It's over to you to steer, George!"

The vardo began to move, and because the ground was flat at this point, it was a nice, steady and well controlled pace. There were a few rocks on the way, but nothing that the vardo, and we, couldn't handle.

Gradually, almost unnoticeably at first, the ground began to slope away from us. I eventually noticed the pace quickening and cried out, "Watch out that it doesn't run away with us!"

Faster and faster it went, like a snowball racing down a hill, until I was running to keep up. The men at the front were not able to run backwards so fast, and had to jump out of the way before a serious accident happened. They joined me on the rope, and the four of us heaved with all our might.

I could now see a belt of trees in front of us, and imagined the horse, vardo, and George smashing straight into them, with who-knows-what in the way of injuries.

Then suddenly, with only seconds to spare, George, turned Comma sharply to the right, so that we then ran across, and not down the slope. This slowed the vardo down enough for us to be able to pull it to a stop.

Young George was the hero of the moment.

"Your quick thinking saved Comma and the vardo. I can't thank you enough."

"Oh, it was nothing," he said, modestly, but I noticed that he blushed with pleasure as he spoke.

"I don't know how you managed it, George. Stopping the vardo is one thing, but this also happens to be the perfect spot for it," I told him. "There's absolutely no need to move it at all. Well done!"

He just smiled back, but I could see he was secretly pleased.

"Come along. We'll allow Romany to settle in," said George's father.

"Thanks for your help and the use of your land, Mr Swalwell," I said to the farmer.

"Are you interested in bird watching, George?" I asked the boy.

"I see lots of birds around the farm", he replied, "but I don't know what they are. I've never been out watching them properly."

"I bet you'd be really good at helping me find nests," I told him. "If it's OK with your father, how would you like to come along tomorrow morning?"

His wide grin said everything. He looked at his father, who just nodded.

"See you in the morning, then," was all I needed to say, and the small party walked off in the direction of the farm.

Firstly, I had to secure the vardo, so I looked around for some large stones and wedged them beneath the wheels, as I always do. Now that the vardo was safe, and not likely to roll away, I could take a better look around.

Further down the slope, behind the belt of trees, I could hear the river chuckling over some rocks. It seemed an ideal spot all round; the ground was flat, the trees sheltered the area from wind, and there was a supply of water close by.

Although I didn't know how I could have missed it on the way down, perhaps it was the excitement, not far from the vardo was a small red-brick cottage. It didn't look as though it was lived-in as there were no curtains at the windows, and some of them were boarded over. I made a mental note to ask George about it sometime.

A short distance away I could see quite a large heap of stones, as though they had been piled-up by some giant hand. I added this to my list of questions for another time.

For now, it was time to organise the inside of the vardo, as the bouncing around it had received had scattered some of my belongings about. Luckily, I always stow the breakable items very carefully, so no real harm had been done. It was the work of just twenty minutes to have everything back in its proper place. In a small caravan, you have to be well organised, otherwise life would quickly become unbearable.

The evening drew to a close as I cooked my supper. Afterwards, I sat on the vardo steps watching Raq and Meg explore the area. By the way they were constantly stopping to sniff, I could tell that a whole host of creatures spent time around this place and I planned to see as many of them as possible over the coming weeks.

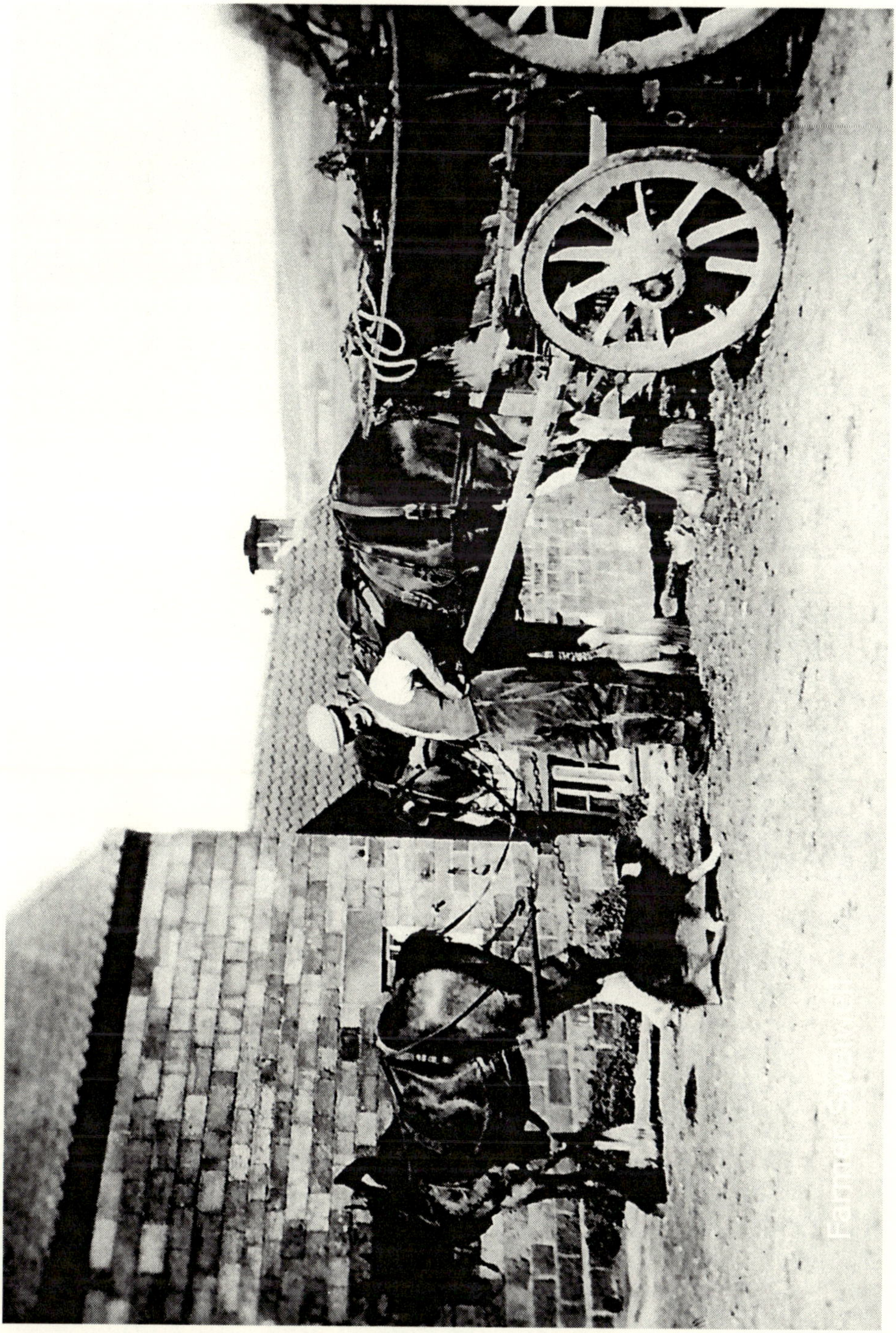
Farm

Chapter 5

George and I visit the owls

The sun was barely up when I was awoken by Raq and Meg loudly barking. I knew right away that someone was about.

"I know you're there," I yelled, pulling on my clothes, hoping this might be enough to frighten off the intruder.

I flung the door open wide and the two dogs rushed out, ready to do battle if necessary.

They ran around the side of the vardo, out of my sight, and the barking stopped quite as suddenly as it had started.

Coming down the steps I was greeted with, "Hello, Romany."

"George; it's you," was my reply. "You gave us the fright of our lives. You're very early; it can't be more than half-past four!"

"I couldn't sleep," he said simply. "I'm sorry for scaring you. By gum, your dogs are sharp."

"They look out for me," I informed him.

He went on to ask various questions about the dogs; their ages, their names and where I'd got them. It seemed he knew farmer Horton and his wife quite well; their dogs, too. He had never seen a cocker spaniel before, but border collies were very common around these parts.

"Every farm has at least one," he told me.

I enquired whether he'd had breakfast, to which he responded, "No, Romany, there was no time."

"But it's only four-thirty," I laughed.

"I didn't want you to go without me," was his answer.

"I always keep my promises," I said. "Come on; breakfast first, then bird watching!"

After we'd eaten, and the dishes were washed and cleared away, I asked George what birds were around the farm.

"We've got some hens," he said, helpfully.

"Not quite what I had in mind, George. I meant wild birds!"

"Oh, I see. We've got some owls in the barn. Is that what you mean, Romany?"

"Exactly, George. I bet your father welcomes them, doesn't he?"

"They take the mice that do a lot of damage. My Dad say's they've always got a home as long as he's on the farm."

"Do you think it would be alright for us to take a look, George?"

"I think it should be," he replied. "We can always ask my Dad when we get there."

I got my binoculars from the vardo and shut the dogs inside. I didn't know whether they would be wanted at the farm, so thought it was safer to leave them behind for my first visit.

George led the way across the slope and all the way he asked questions about me, the vardo, the dogs and bird watching. I was quite exhausted by the time we reached the farmyard!

Between the very few gaps in his questions I managed to find out that the cottage near to the camp had once been owned by a miner and his family, and that the heap of stones was all that was left of his iron-ore mine. When the ore had run out, he had simply moved on to try his luck elsewhere.

I waited, while George went into the farmhouse to see his father. While he was away, I took the opportunity to glance around.

I was standing in a fairly large rectangular yard, with the house and barns forming the boundary. The yard surface was roughly cobbled, and sloped down away from the entrance on the roadside, where I had first met George yesterday.

The buildings were constructed from a light-coloured stone, which looked very attractive in the early-morning light. Any exposed woodwork, doors, window frames, etc., were painted a dark red, almost maroon, colour, but the paint was clearly old as it was flaking off.

My inspection was interrupted by George who announced, "Dad says it will be fine to photograph the owls, so long as we don't disturb them. He needs them to nest in the barn because of all the good they do."

"I quite understand, George, but I always take care not to disturb any bird," I nodded.

I went on, "The sign of a good birdwatcher and photographer is that nothing at all is disturbed; not even the area *around* the nest."

"How can you do that?" enquired George.

"It takes care and practice," I informed him. "Whenever we go out together, I'll show you how," I promised.

"Shall we go into the barn?" George asked.

"Show me the way, then," I told him.

Before I could stop him he ran to an adjacent building and flung open the large door, which made a loud squeal as the obviously dry hinges protested. As he did so, out from the small hole that was set into the top of the barn flew the resident barn owl.

George didn't see it go, but I told him about it, saying, "See what I mean about not disturbing the birds?"

"I'm sorry, Romany," he said apologetically. "I didn't mean to frighten it off. Will it come back?"

"Of course it will, but we shouldn't hang around, in case we keep it from its owlets."

"Owlets?" George said, raising an eyebrow.

"Just a name for young owls," I informed him. "Can you quickly show me the nest?" I enquired.

"Up behind yonder beam," he pointed.

In the gloom of the barn, as my eyes adjusted to the low light level, I could just see the fluffy tops of three heads bobbing and weaving about in an alcove high up in the roof-space.

"I can't see any twigs," whispered George.

"That's because they don't use any nesting material," I responded. "They're one of very few British birds that just lay their eggs on a flat patch, without anything surrounding them or holding them together."

We stayed for just another minute or two and then went outside into the yard where we were both temporarily dazzled by the sunshine.

"Let's move away," I suggested. "It will give the adult time to get back to her young. Why don't we sit on that step over there and watch?"

We moved about twenty yards away, across from the barn, and sat down. Just as on our walk from the vardo, George bombarded me with questions, this time about barn owls.

He asked so many that I can't remember them all, but I do recall:

"Was it a male or female that you saw flying away?" I wasn't able to say, as they aren't that easy to tell apart; especially with only a fleeting glimpse.

"Do they fly south for the winter?"

"No, they don't migrate."

"What colour are their eggs?"

"White."

"Can we take an egg from the nest later?"

"By the size of the owlets there wouldn't be any eggs left in the nest. Anyway, to take an egg away from any bird is a cruel thing, and barn owls are in danger of becoming extinct."

After almost ten minutes of questioning, I said, "Here it comes!"

I had spotted the bird flying into the yard area from across the fields, roughly in the direction of the vardo.

This time I had a good look at it through my binoculars. It was slightly greyer in colour than many barn owls I had seen, so I took it to be a female and told George. In its feet it was carrying something small and brown, which I could see was a field mouse.

"She's got herself some breakfast," George remarked.

"Oh, that's not likely," I told him. "She'll see to her young, first. It's her instinct."

"My Mum makes our breakfast before she has her own," observed George. "It must be her instinct, too!"

"Perhaps she just wants to get you off to school!" I laughed.

"The nest is in a really tricky spot for taking a photograph," I commented. "My only suggestion is that I climb up on the hay-bales and set my camera on top. It may not be close enough, though."

"There's a ladder in the other barn," said George. I can get it," he offered.

"I think we should leave it undisturbed for a while," I proposed. "We don't want those young birds to be abandoned, do we?"

"Do you mean she might leave them for good?" George asked, concerned.

"There is that risk if we spend too much time around her territory," I warned him. "You can take me down to the river for now, and I can think of how we can organise our owl photography. I'm keen to get a really good shot of the young birds, and we might need to do it when the mother is away."

We went back to the vardo where both dogs greeted us. I noticed that Raq would say a quick 'hello' to George, and then come back to me. Meg, however, was clearly taken with George, and spent more time fussing over him. This didn't surprise me as I would describe Raq as a 'one man dog.'

I collected my fishing rod, net and an assortment of dry flies, artificial flies made from feathers that I would use to tempt the brown trout onto my hook, and later into my pan!

George had been fishing before, he told me, and was delighted to describe to me all those really big fish that had escaped him, in the way that all good fishermen recount.

He led me down the steep slope towards the river and I reflected on what might have been had the vardo continued straight ahead instead of George's quick thinking avoiding disaster.

After just ten minutes we reached some trees where, through the gaps, I could see the river.

"It's easier to get to over here," George suggested.

We turned right, parallel to the trees and I immediately noticed some patches of reddish, disturbed earth, with large, black holes disappearing underground. I stopped and carefully examined the ground surrounding one of the holes. From the footprints in the mud, I knew that the disturbance was created by a badger – five distinct toes and a large pad behind were the clue.

A little way beyond the badger sett was a barbed wire fence. I could see a trail through the grass, running beneath the fence, so went over to look. Sure enough, caught on the wire were a few strands of grey hair indicating that a badger had passed that way. Another mental note was entered on my list of birds and animals to watch. I would run out of time at this rate, before I had seen half of the things on my list.

We spent several hours in a deep pool at a bend in the river, and with some success. I managed to catch two brown trout and George netted one.

"They should make quite a supper," I remarked, pleased with our triumph. However, some days when you fish, you catch nothing at all. Sometimes you don't even raise the fish's interest, but that isn't the point. To spend time so close to nature, to remain so still that even the deer that comes to drink at the water's edge does not see you, to hear the music of the river as it makes the sound of a million tiny bells, is the reward; fish for supper is the bonus.

As we climbed the hill to the camp, I reflected on the time spent in silence at the river. I'd had the chance to develop a plan for photographing the young owls, which I hadn't yet shared with George. There was plenty of time for that. We were all hungry; George, me, the dogs.

Back at the vardo, I lit the fire and George made polite signs that he should go. I could tell, however, that he didn't really want to.

"Why don't you ask your Mother if you can eat with me," I suggested.

"Really? Can I?" he spluttered.

"Of course; three trout's too much for me. I need help!"

He shot away across the fields and was back within ten minutes.

"My Mum say's it's OK, as long as I'm not a nuisance," he panted.

"Good. Help me fry these, then," I told him.

I had filleted the fish while he was away and we simply popped the trout into a large frying pan over the fire, and within a few minutes we had a tasty meal.

We had settled down to eat our supper, when I introduced George to my plan.

"Tomorrow, I'd like to get that photograph," I started. "We'll wait for the adult to leave the barn, I'll climb up on the hay, and you can watch out for her returning and warn me when you see her."

"I wanted to watch you take the photograph," complained George.

"If you do a good job on lookout, I'll let you take a shot of your own," I offered.

"I've never used a camera before. That would be wonderful," he gushed.

"Let's look forward to tomorrow, then," I concluded.

Chapter 6

We go fishing for owls!

Just as on the previous morning, I was awoken by the two dogs announcing the arrival of George. As soon as I opened the door he greeted me with an excited, "I've seen it, Romany!"

"Tell me exactly what you saw," I requested.

"One of the adult birds flew out of the barn just as I came out of the farm, and I ran straight here," he told me, rather breathlessly.

"Well, that sounds like good news," I replied. "They must be feeding the young during daylight hours, which means we can get set-up for some photographs."

George dashed around excitedly, getting more in the way than helping. In the end, I gave him my large wooden camera tripod to carry, saying, "Here, George. It would be a great help if you could take this."

He almost stumbled under the weight, but manfully held on to it, despite the struggle.

Meanwhile, I packed my plate camera and several glass plates into a haversack I use for my photography.

My old camera isn't like any of the modern lightweight instruments you see today. It is probably the equivalent of ten small cameras in size and weighs as much as forty of them! Nor is it digital and it doesn't take film. For every photograph I take, I have to carry a specially treated glass plate, which, of course, is easily broken.

Between us we managed to stumble our way across the fields to Cragg Farm, where we were glad to unload the weight from our shoulders. It was another warm morning and we were both drenched in sweat after our efforts.

"Let's take a rest and just watch for a while," I suggested to George, who seemed quite happy to follow my lead.

"I'll nip inside and make us a cup of tea," he said, helpfully.

"You do that, George. I won't forget you if the owl arrives," I promised.

However, ten minutes passed by and George arrived with two large brown mugs of steaming tea but there was still no sign of the adult owl.

"I was just thinking that we should stay here, allow the owl to feed the young, and when it leaves again we know we have a while to set up the equipment."

George was obviously quite pleased with this arrangement, for he sank down on the bare cobbles with his tea and simply nodded. I suspected that two very early mornings, followed by the effort of carrying the heavy equipment, had taken its toll. Sure enough, within five minutes his head had fallen to one side and he was fast asleep; he hadn't even touched his tea!

Not much more than five minutes went by when across the fields I saw a white shape fluttering towards us.

"George," I whispered. "George; wake up! It's here."

Rather slowly, he lifted his head.

"I wasn't asleep," he muttered, "I was just resting my eyes."

"That's what everyone says," I chuckled. "Anyway, the adult is on its way back."

We could see it making a slightly erratic line for the barn. In a few seconds it increased height and shot straight up towards the small hole at the top of the barn. For a moment I thought it might miss and hit the wall, but this was an experienced bird. Very accurately, it landed square in the centre of the black opening, shuffled about a bit and was gone. I was sure it had been carrying a small vole in its talons.

"I was worried it was going to hurt itself," George said.

"You know, I thought exactly the same," I confessed. "We need to give it a little more credit!"

"What happens now?" George asked.

"Simple. We wait," I told him. "Bird watching and bird photography are eighty percent patience."

For the next twenty minutes George asked many questions about the birds I had seen on my travels. What was the rarest, the smallest, the most difficult to find. Just as on the previous occasion, his questions left me exhausted.

I was rescued by the owl emerging from the barn. It looked around, its head swivelling as though it was on a pivot.

"It can almost turn its head in a complete circle," George hissed to me.

"All owls can do that," I informed him.

A few moments later it launched itself from its perch in the owl hole and was gone across the fields.

Barn Owl

"I've seen owls lots of times," George said, "but I never noticed that they could do that before."

"A good bird watcher sees the behaviour as well as the bird," was my reply. "Come on, we've no time to lose," I added.

We picked up the camera equipment and carried it into the barn. I climbed on to a bale of hay and asked George to begin passing me each item. I then climbed onto a higher bale. George got up onto the lower one and we repeated the process.

Ten minutes later, all of the equipment was on the highest bale. However, I was concerned that the adult owl would return while we were setting up, so I told George to climb down again, and we would wait outside.

We again sat in the farmyard and within minutes the owl was back. This time I got a clear look at the mouse it was carrying.

Several minutes later it appeared again and flew away.

We rushed to the barn, climbed the bales and I began to set the camera on the tripod.

The young owls eyed us with suspicion and kept up their hissing as we worked quickly in the rising heat.

When all was ready I took a look through the back of the camera. I could see nothing of any interest! The owls were squashed back into the alcove, totally out of range of the camera.

"It's no use," I complained. "Unless they come out of hiding, we won't be able to photograph them."

George answered, "Oh no! I've been looking forward to getting a picture of them ever since you came to the farm."

"Let's leave things here to let the birds get used to them," I suggested. "We'll go back down and make a plan." I could see that poor George was really upset and even thought he might cry.

Outside, I racked my brains as to how we might get a decent photograph. If only there was some way of getting them nearer and away from their alcove, yet without them coming to any harm.

We must have sat for an hour, talking over possible ideas, and in the meantime the adult bird made two further visits.

We were going round in circles, and in exasperation George remarked, "I think I like fishing better than photography."

"Well done, George," I shouted.

George jumped.

"What have I done?" he asked.

"You've given me an idea, that's what," I cried.

"I only said that fishing was better than photography," he said, puzzled.

"We'll fish for the owlets," I said triumphantly.

"I still don't understand what you mean, Romany." He looked at me strangely.

I explained my idea. "If we get a stick and put something on the end that they might cling to, we could bring the stick out, take a shot of them, and put them back. We wouldn't need to handle them, so our scent wouldn't be obvious to the adult when it gets back."

"Do you think it would work?" George enquired.

"It's certainly worth a try," I told him. "Can you get a stick from somewhere and perhaps some sort of cloth to wrap around the end?"

"I'll have a look in the house," he said, excitedly. Suddenly all his enthusiasm had returned. He was gone in a flash, leaving me to think over my idea. It just might work.

George was gone for a little while, but then emerged from the farmhouse door and ran across the yard carrying an old walking stick and what looked like a thin piece of brown-coloured cloth. When he reached me I could see it was a ladies nylon stocking.

"Whatever will your Mother say?" I asked, sternly.

"She won't say anything," George responded with a chuckle, "It's my Grannie's!"

"All the same, George, we need permission to use it. It will probably get damaged; owls have sharp talons."

"Grannie says it doesn't matter. I told her it was an emergency!"

"I hope she's as understanding when she hears how we've used it," I remarked.

I wrapped the stocking around the end of the walking stick and tied it in place, so that it formed a pad.

"Right, George; here we go," I said.

We swarmed up to the top of the bales and I showed George how to operate the camera. I inserted a glass plate, saying, "We'll only get one chance at this; when I say now, press the shutter button."

I lay down on my stomach and inched my way forward until I could reach the alcove with the walking stick. Slowly and gently, I pushed the stick into the dark recess and hoped for the best. After what seemed like an age, but which was probably only a minute, I felt something move on the end of the stick. Almost afraid to breathe, I began to withdraw the stick, taking care not to jerk it or make any sudden movement.

As it emerged into the lighter area of the hay bales, I could see an owlet had attached itself to the stocking and was gripping it tightly with its claws.

I pulled it past me into the zone of the camera – it was hissing at me all of the time.

Disconcertingly, I recalled the story of the great wildlife photographer, Eric Hosking, who lost an eye when an adult tawny owl attacked him for taking a young bird to be photographed.

I whispered to George, "Press the shutter now." I heard a reassuring click and began to replace the owlet in the alcove.

I withdrew the walking stick, only to find that the bird was still attached! I made five attempts to put it back, on the last occasion shaking the stick until I felt that it had become lighter, indicating that the owlet had rejoined its siblings. I crawled back to George and the camera equipment, and we hastily beat a retreat down to the barn floor. We had detached the camera from the tripod knowing that we could always go back for it later.

"Well, George, that was one picture. Let's hope it was in focus," I said, concerned that we might have to repeat the episode.

Looking at Grannie's stocking, I could see that the owlet's long and sharp claws had torn it to shreds.

"I must apologise in person to your Grandmother," I cautiously said to George.

"Come along to the farmhouse then," he offered.

I followed him in, and he introduced me to an elderly lady with dark hair, which was tied back, and she was wearing wire-rimmed glasses framing her dark eyes. She was knitting a garment as we approached.

"I'm sorry, we've destroyed your stocking," I said, apologetically. "I'll pay for new ones, if you like."

"There's no need," she offered graciously.

"How can I repay you, then" I enquired.

"That won't be necessary – Romany, isn't it?" she asked.

"It is, but I feel so guilty at having damaged it."

"I recognised your voice. We listen to your programmes on the wireless," she informed me, "but I didn't know you were a photographer, too."

I nodded, an idea forming as to how I might repay her for the ruined stocking.

"Why don't I take your photograph, Grannie?" I offered.

"Oh, I don't think so," was all she said.

But George eventually persuaded her, so she went outside where the light was better.

While I climbed back into the barn to recover the tripod, George brought a chair from within the house and I took a very simple photograph of her, sitting just outside the open door. Try as I might, I could not persuade her to put down her knitting, so had to include it in the shot!

George and I then went back to the vardo where I blacked-out the windows and door and developed the two glass plates to make negatives from which I made two paper prints; one of the owl, which I gave to George to keep, and one of Grannie, on which I wrote 'From Romany to Grannie, 1937.'

George ran off with both photographs, pleased as Punch with his own efforts. His very first photograph was excellent, showing the young barn owl in some detail.

The signed photograph of Grannie took pride of place on the family sideboard for many years, and is still treasured by George and his own family today.

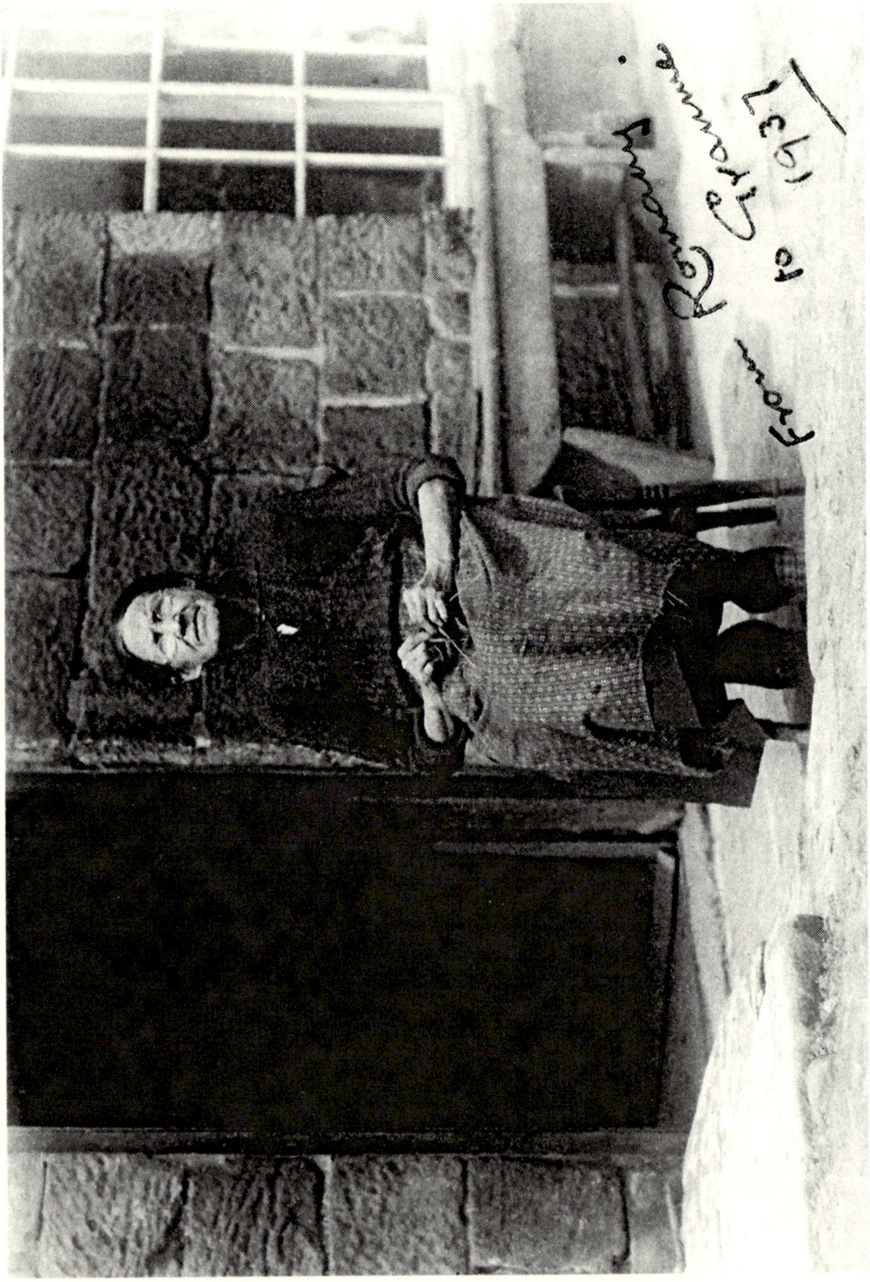

Chapter 7

The Cottage

By now I was confident in leaving Meg completely free to run around as she pleased. She had needed so little training in comparison to Raq, who I thought would never keep to heel. Perhaps it was because she came from well-trained working parents. I always feel that the sight of a dog taking its owner for a walk, instead of the other way around, makes me think that not enough effort has been put into their training.

My thoughts turned to the day ahead and how I might spend the time. Just as I was forming a plan, Meg gave a little bark and bounded off. This was a sure sign that George was nearby. Sure enough, a few minutes later, the pair appeared. George greeted me with, "Hello, Romany. What are your plans for today?"

"I had thought that it might be nice to take a walk along the river bank," I suggested, adding, "How about joining me?"

As usual, George was ready for any adventure.

"I can take you along the miner's track," he offered.

"Miner's track? What kind of mine?" I enquired.

"Iron," George said. "The miner used to dig just around here and take the ore down the track to the railway."

"Where did it go from there?" I asked him.

"I don't know exactly, but somewhere in the North East, where it went into the making of steel," he answered.

"I suppose it's just possible that the very railway lines the ore was transported on could be made from the stuff he dug from the ground," I thought aloud.

"How would he get it to the steel mill if the railway wasn't built?" George challenged.

"Good point, George," I praised him. "Which came first, the chicken or the egg?"

"What chicken?" George asked, looking puzzled.

"It's just a saying," I told him. "You use it when you're not sure which thing happens first. We still don't understand whether a hen produces an egg before the chick appears inside it, or if it's the other way around."

George gave me a blank look. "You've lost me," he remarked. What's a hen's egg got to do with steel railway lines?"

"Hmm! I can see I'm just making things worse," I confessed. "Let's go for that walk instead," I quickly offered.

"That's best," was George's short response!

So we made our way through the trees, always keeping the sounds of the river ahead of us. Raq, as always, ran ahead, sniffed a patch of grass, raced back to me with his tail wagging, and was off again in search of who knows what. Meg, however, stayed close to us, but in particular to George, nuzzling his hand occasionally, as he bent slightly to pat her head.

George led the way and all the while the river sounds, faint at first, could be heard getting stronger. It was as well I had him as a guide, as this wasn't the same route I had taken when I went fishing.

Without warning, the river came into view. I had a feeling we were much further downstream than the fishing spot. There was a sharp bend, which left a large area of very damp ground.

"This might be interesting," I ventured. "The plants, insects and animals are quite different on damp soil, compared to dry. Let's take a closer look."

We wandered over and I set George a task. "First, I want you to find three plants that you wouldn't find on really dry soil."

"But what if I don't know their names?" he protested.

"Don't worry about what they're called," I replied. "If I can't name them, we'll check in this little book I have." I produced a guide to wild flowers from my large poacher's pocket.

He spotted one almost straight away, saying, "Here's one I haven't seen before, so I suppose it must be a damp-lover."

Ragged Robin

"Well done, George! That's a good start. It's called ragged robin."

I joined him and we examined the plant together.

The pink flowers were, as you might imagine, rather ragged, causing George to remark, "I think something's eaten them."

"Sorry to disappoint you; that's exactly the way they're meant to be."

"But it's even short of leaves; what a poor excuse for a plant!" he cried.

"You mustn't judge it by other plants," I said. "Not everything is showy in the natural world. That was a great effort; now see if you can spot another."

He moved a little way up the bank, scouring the ground as he went.

"I'm really struggling, Romany," he reported.

"I think the soil is really acidic around here," I told him. "That may mean that there's a rather special plant about."

"What am I looking for? Can't I have a clue?"

"Alright, George. It's a very low-growing plant, with tiny hairs on the leaves. The tips of the hairs are reddish in colour and are very sticky when you touch them."

"Sticky? Why's that, then?" he asked me.

"Find one first, then I'll explain."

Some minutes passed, and he was unusually silent, completely absorbed in his quest for the plant I had described.

Suddenly, both dogs gave a startled yelp as he shouted, "Got one!"

When I had checked he was right, I praised him, saying, "That's the second; you are doing so well."

"Tell me about it then," was his anxious statement. "Why does it have those sticky blobs on the end of the tiny stalks?

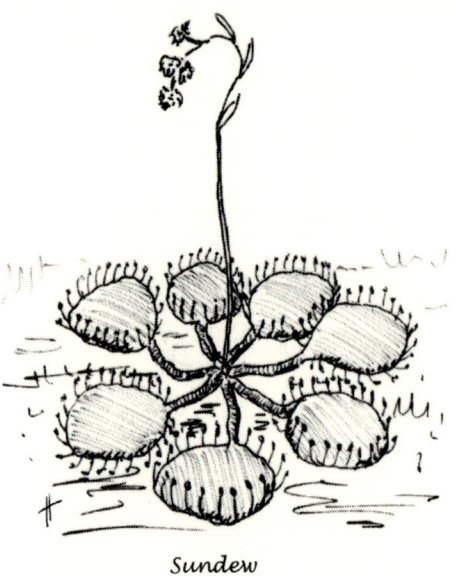

Sundew

"Well, it's quite a gruesome story. Do you understand what 'carnivorous' means?"

He shook his head.

"It means 'meat eating.'"

"But what's that got to do with this tiny plant?" he asked.

I went on, "In the area it lives there usually aren't many nutrients – chemicals that most plants feed on from the soil – so it has to find food in other ways."

His face was a picture as he began to realise where this might be leading.

"When tiny flies land on the sticky leaves they find they can't release themselves – a bit like the flypaper that your dad uses in the stables where the horses are kept. The small hairs can move and they close over the fly, trapping it completely. The plant contains special chemicals called enzymes, which then help it to digest the fly. Gruesome, isn't it?"

"Who'd have thought; a man-eating plant," he exaggerated.

"Well, not quite," I answered. "Surprisingly, it's got a rather lovely name – it's a sundew. Now, finally, plant number three. I suggest you go to the edge of the trees and smell."

He followed my directions and was soon sniffing the air by the woods.

"There's a really strong smell here; a bit like onions," he called.

"That's the one; sniff it out, George," I encouraged him.

"Is it the one with the white flowers?" he asked.

"It is indeed."

"I don't like the smell," he said, wrinkling his nose in disgust.

Wild Garlic

"Some people call it wild garlic, others, ramsons; either way it's a member of the onion family. You can eat the leaves, but the taste gets less strong when you cook it."

"No thank you," was his curt reply.

"Why don't we go back to the vardo, George," I suggested. "That smell has made me hungry."

"I don't want anything with onions, thanks," he smiled.

He again led the way, but this time taking a slightly different route. When we emerged from the wood into the clearing where the vardo lay, it was from the opposite side to the one we had left by. I again spotted the cottage that I'd seen when I'd first arrived at the farm.

"That place looks interesting, George," I said.

"Haunted!" was the single-word reply.

"Oh come on; you don't believe that, surely?" I asked.

"Everyone at school says it is, although I haven't seen anything myself."

"Whose cottage is it, then?" I enquired.

"It did belong to the miner; look; you can see the heap of stones he left behind."

Sure enough, there was a large mound of broken stones, mainly rusty red in colour, caused by the iron we'd spoken about earlier in the day.

We got closer to the cottage and I could see now that it was empty. Most of the windows' were boarded over and there were many slates missing from the roof. Grass was sprouting from the gutters and the whole place had a sad, neglected feel about it.

Suddenly, I realised I was alone. Neither George, nor the dogs had followed me.

"Come on, there's nothing to be afraid of," I called.

Reluctantly, George ambled over to me.

"I'm not sure about this," he muttered, quietly, almost under his breath.

"Let me prove to you that it's alright." I spoke quite firmly.

Pushing against the old front door, it suddenly gave way with a squeak, which caused him to jump. We stepped inside what had evidently been the living room. The paint was peeling from the walls and ceiling and there was a damp smell about the place.

I broke the silence. "Hard to imagine the miner living here. It's been empty for so long."

"He never lived here while I've been alive," George whispered.

We moved through to the kitchen. The old cooking range was there, rusting now, but obviously someone's pride and joy in times gone by. Then, without warning, there was an almighty crash from an upstairs room and George was out of the door like a rocket!

I dashed upstairs to the room above the kitchen, where I found one of the few un-boarded windows wide open. Strewn across the floor was old hay, feathers and many bird droppings. It was quite obvious that something large had been nesting there and I suspected it was a wood pigeon.

I went downstairs and left the cottage and found George on the far side of the clearing.

"I told you it was haunted," were the first words from his mouth.

"I reckon you're right," I agreed with him.

"You do? Did you see it? Was it awful? What do you think it was?" he asked.

Slowly and deliberately I replied, "I'm sure it was a columba palumbus; in fact, I'm certain."

"Ooh!" he squealed. "Everyone says so – I'm glad I got out when I did."

I looked over his shoulder and said, loudly, "It's behind you now!"

He turned around so fast I thought he might topple over. His head whipped from left to right and finally he said, "I can't see anything; only that old pigeon."

"That," I said triumphantly, "is columba palumbus. Let's get supper!" and led the way back to the vardo.

Chapter 8

A trip to the seaside

Almost a week after the episode at the miner's cottage, George arrived at the vardo with my daily pint of milk. I was quite happy to call for it at the farm, but George insisted that it was his job. I think secretly he wanted to see Meg, who always greeted him with real affection. Raq, also, was happy to see him, but, once he'd said 'hello,' he quickly lost interest, whereas Meg would continue to fuss over him.

"I'm off down to the sea, today," I informed him. "Are you doing anything special?"

"I promised Dad I'd help him clear out the woodshed," George said, rather regretfully, I thought.

"What sort of things will you see?" he enquired.

"Well, you can never be certain, but I expect gannets, which I'd like to photograph; perhaps some pipits on the cliff top, and anything the tide has washed-up onto the shore."

George was becoming increasingly anxious-looking as I described the possibilities. Finally, with an, "I'll just go and see Dad," he was off like a hare in the direction of the farm. Turning back, he shouted, "Don't leave without me, Romany," which I acknowledged with a wave.

Almost half-an-hour passed as I tidied around the camp area. Then, suddenly, Meg, who had been dozing beneath the vardo, leapt to her feet and ran towards George who was approaching us, although he was still over a hundred yards away. A dog's senses never cease to amaze me. Although I had no idea that he was on his way back, Meg had heard George a long way off, and she'd been asleep!

He opened with an apology. "I'm sorry I took so long, Romany. I was afraid you'd gone. Dad made me chop some wood before I could come back."

"Are you certain it's alright to come with me?" I asked.

"So long as I'm not a nuisance, Dad said," was his response.

"You're never a nuisance, George. Your questions make me think very hard about what I know. I rediscover things I'd forgotten, so you're always welcome to join me on my expeditions."

While George played with Meg, I made some sandwiches and a large flask of tea. It was quite some way to the coast and I knew we would be away for the whole day.

"Can we take the dogs with us, Romany?" George asked.

"I don't see why not," I told him, which pleased him greatly.

When everything we needed was loaded into my haversack, we set off on foot. Our way led us through the farmyard and out onto the lane down which I had travelled from the orchard. It seemed such a long time ago that we had been flooded-out and a disaster had only just been avoided. No point in dwelling on the past, though.

Along the lane we came across Farmer Horton repairing a wall. He greeted us with a cheery, "How do, Romany?"

We spent a few minutes chatting about the weather, my new campsite, the price of lambs and general farming topics. I could sense that George was wanting to be off, so we said a quick goodbye to the farmer and we were off again.

Some time later, we were drawing close to a long hedge, when I told George to stop and listen.

"Tell me what you can hear?" I instructed.

After a moment, he spoke. "There's a cow away yonder," he said, brightly.

"That's not really what I meant," I replied. "What is the bird you can hear calling?"

We stood stock still for a while; even the dogs sat and listened.

"There. That wheezy sound," I was able to say at last.

"I don't know what it is, Romany," was George's reply.

"Some people say that it sounds like 'a little bit of bread and no cheese.' Personally, I'm not sure I agree, but it's a useful way to remember it."

"I can hear the long note at the end of the call," George said, adding, "But it doesn't sound much like 'cheese' to me, either."

I passed the binoculars to George who took a moment to find the bird in question. When he found it, he gave a startled, "Romany; it's a canary!"

"Not quite, George, but I admit it's very yellow in colour. But look at the shape – tell me what you see."

"It's fatter than a canary," he observed. "It's really more like a sparrow. I can see some brown on it, too. What is it, Romany?"

"It's called a yellowhammer," I informed him.

"Well I don't think I've ever seen anything as bright, without it being in a cage," exclaimed George.

"I know what you mean. But we do have some really gaudy birds in this country."

I told him about the kingfisher and even the humble starling, which, in the right light, takes on the appearance of oil on water.

Yellowhammer

"We'll never reach the sea if we carry on at this rate," I said, concerned that we still had some distance to cover. So on we went, a little faster than before.

After another hour we were in sight of the cliffs.

"At last," George sighed. "I thought we'd be walking forever."

We found a steep path that led down to the sea. On either side the towering cliffs blocked out the sunlight, and the air was quite cool. We were glad to reach the bottom and find ourselves on a long, sunny stretch of sandy beach. The dogs seemed happy, too. Raq ran off to be closely followed by Meg. They yapped excitedly at each other, showing no sign that they'd just walked five or six miles.

"They make me feel tired just watching them," George remarked.

"I know what will revive you – lunch," I remarked, taking off my haversack.

We opened the sandwiches I had made and I poured us each a cup of tea from the flask.

As we were eating I was looking out to sea. In the distance I could just make out half a dozen large, very white birds. I took out the binoculars and had a better look. My suspicions were correct – they were gannets, making for the cliff tops over to our left. I made a mental note to go there another day to obtain some photographs.

When we had both finished I suggested a walk down to the tide line, to which George readily agreed. We were soon at the water's edge, eagerly searching the sand for shells.

After a few minutes ticked by I noticed the quiet; George hadn't asked any questions. I glanced at him to find that he was staring ahead of us, hardly looking at the sand at all. I said nothing for a moment and just watched him. We passed several interesting shells and he completely ignored them. Eventually my curiosity got the better of me.

"A penny for them," I broke the eerie silence at last.

"Sorry, Romany. I'm miles way," he replied.

"What's on your mind then, George?" I enquired, fully expecting he might want to talk about some difficult problem that he was facing.

"I was wondering," he began, "why that bird over yonder has hold of a carrot."

I looked along the tide line and saw what he meant.

"Well, you had me fooled," I informed him. "I expected you might have some huge problem you needed solving; instead you ask me a question about a bird!"

"But you haven't said why it's carrying a carrot," George pleaded.

"The simple answer is that it isn't!"

"That doesn't make sense," he frowned.

"I'll explain. It's called an oystercatcher, George, and that's not a carrot, but its beak," I explained. However, it's actually far more than just a beak," I went on. "Have you ever seen one of those penknives with lots of different blades, all for doing different jobs?" He nodded. "This is the bird-world equivalent. It's a three-in-one, handy tool." I could see I had his full attention, so I gave him the story.

Oyster Catcher

"The reason the beak is so long is to enable the bird to dig deep into the mud for the shellfish it eats. That's tool number one."

"What's tool number two?" he interrupted.

"The tip of the beak is very sensitive and when it digs around it can feel the shell it's looking for."

"And three?" he asked, anxiously.

"It's a pair of pliers and a chisel."

"But that makes four," he retorted.

"You know, I suppose it does, but who's counting?" I laughed.

"So why does it need a pair of pliers and a chisel?" He was back on his old form now.

By way of an answer I walked on a few yards and picked up a cockle shell. I handed it to George, saying, "Let me see you open it."

He grasped the shell in both hands and tried to pry it open. First one way, then another, he twisted it. By the look on his face and the whiteness of his fingers he was trying his hardest. Finally, exasperated, he said, "It's no use, Romany. I can't do it." He looked disgusted with himself.

"Don't worry, George, I've never managed it, either."

His response was, "I can see why it needs pliers and a chisel; otherwise it would starve!" and he gave a wry smile.

We walked on a little way and I pointed to a dead fish lying by my feet.

"Ooh! What's that?" cried George

"It's a piece of sandpaper."

"You are talking in some riddles today, Romany. It's a dead fish, not sandpaper."

"Ah, but it's a dogfish, George. In old times, people used to dry-out its skin and it's then so rough that it can be used like sandpaper."

"Well I never. Dad has to buy his from Whitby."

Just then the oystercatcher and a host of other birds took to the sky. Meg and Raq were bounding towards us. When they reached us I said, "A couple of regular mobile bird-scarers, aren't you? I could rent you out to farmers who find that scarecrows don't work!"

Yet again I noticed Meg fussing over George who was playfully tickling her behind the ears.

"You've got a friend for life," I remarked.

He just smiled back, saying, "I shall miss her when you move on." He turned away, deep in thought.

Not quite knowing what to say next, I looked up at the sky. The sun was much higher than I expected, so I took out my pocket watch. It was almost five o'clock.

"We're never going to make it before dark," I said, concerned.

I thought carefully about what we might do; an idea forming in my mind.

"We haven't photographed the gannets," George reminded me.

"Sandsend," I said, thinking aloud.

"I know Sandsend," George replied. "I think it's just along the coast from here. But what's that got to do with getting home before dark?"

"I have some friends there. If we stayed with them, we could telephone home to tell your Mum and Dad what's happening."

"But we don't have a telephone, Romany. Dad says they're a waste of money because no-one we know has one."

"If everybody said that, George, then it would be completely true. Each person would wait for somebody else to get one. But that doesn't solve the problem. Do any of your neighbours have a telephone?"

"Mr Horton has one; where you first parked the vardo," he volunteered.

"That will do. I'm sure he'll get a message to Cragg Farm. Let's see, I reckon we head north from here and get up off the beach at the next gorge."

Twenty minutes walking saw us up on the road that ran along the cliff top. Parallel to the road was a railway line. In the distance we could see a cluster of cottages nestling against the hillside.

"I'm sure that's Sandsend," George said. "I've been there three times, I think."

"Well, the house we want is in a tiny little street. I don't know its name, but I'll recognise it when I see it."

Reaching the outskirts of the village, the road took a very sharp left bend, followed immediately by a stone bridge. We passed beneath an iron viaduct carrying the railway high above our heads.

I was now confident of my route, and in just two more minutes we were knocking on the door of a tiny fisherman's cottage, just back from the sea front.

In a few moments the light from an oil lamp showed through the glass pane of the front door. It was dark in the tiny alleyway, despite the early hour.

The door was opened by a small man wearing a heavy navy-blue sweater. Clearly the warm weather hadn't stopped the fashion-habit of a lifetime!

I greeted him with, "Billy, you old goat; how are you?"

"Romany, is that you? I'd heard you were in this neck of the woods. Where's Raq?"

At the mention of his name, Raq pushed his way forward and licked Billy's hand. Meg, though, stayed back, nuzzling George's hand for reassurance.

I introduced the boy, saying, "Billy McLean, this is my young friend, George. My vardo is on his father's farm, near Sleights.

"Hello, George," greeted Billy. "Which farm is it?"

"Cragg Farm, sir," George replied, politely.

"Bless you, there's no need to 'sir' me. I've known you're old Dad for years; your name's Swalwell isn't it?"

George nodded in response.

Billy invited us in with a, "Come in, come in, dogs an' all. The more the merrier."

"So, to what do we owe the pleasure?" Billy enquired after we'd sat down in his small living room.

"To tell the truth, Billy, we've stayed on the beach too long and it's far too late to get back to the farm tonight. There are two things; a telephone and rooms for the night."

"I can do one, but not the other," laughed Billy. "You are welcome to bed down here for the night, but I don't have a telephone. You're in luck on both counts, though, because Mrs Norman, two doors away, has just had one fitted. Her son who lives in Grosmont paid for it."

While George fed the dogs, I went with Billy to make the call. Mrs Norman kindly allowed me to use her telephone, telling me that she wasn't sure how to make a call.

"I know how to answer it, though," she said. "Whenever our Wilf rings, I say, 'Norman household, here; how can I help?' It always makes him chuckle."

I made the call, and Farmer Horton promised to ride over to Cragg Farm on his bike, saying it would take 'nowt but a minute.'

Back at Billy's cottage, I found George and the dogs snuggled-up together, but Raq came over to me as I walked in.

Billy made us some supper while George and I spoke of how we would photograph the gannets.

After our meal was over and the dishes washed and cleared away, Billy entertained us with his stories of his fishing-days, spent far out in the North Sea.

The food, warmth and soft glow of the oil lamps began to work their magic and, try as he might, George couldn't prevent his head from nodding. Every now and again, he would sit bolt upright as though nothing had happened. Finally, after what must have been the twentieth occasion, I said, "Time we turned in. We've another early start tomorrow."

George looked extremely grateful as we made up his bed downstairs.

As I was about to go up the small staircase to the tiniest of bedrooms at the back of the cottage, George made a request.

"Romany; do you think Meg might like to stay down here, with me?"

I gave a simple reply. "Why don't you ask her yourself?"

"Meg!" called George.

She bounded back downstairs and leapt straight onto his bed.

"I think the answer's yes!" I chuckled, and made my way to my room.

Chapter 9

The gannets, at last!

I was awoken by a soft tapping on the door of my small bedroom. By now I had become used to George's habit of rising early in the morning and today he hadn't let me down. It was just after five o'clock when I glanced at the wall clock.

"I'll be with you soon," I whispered, not wishing to disturb Billy. However, I'd been downstairs no more than a few minutes when he came into the tiny kitchen.

"Can't be photographing gannets on an empty stomach," he laughed, and set-to making our breakfast.

Forty minutes later we were outside the tiny cottage thanking him for his hospitality.

"Look me up again when you're next in Sandsend," Billy offered.

"Of course I will, Billy," I said, "although I don't expect I'll be back for a while."

George and I, closely followed by Raq and Meg, headed north from the village. Our way soon led to the cliff top and within just a mile or two we were close to the colony of gannets that nested there. Billy had made us a packet of sandwiches and a flask of tea, so we were self-sufficient for the day.

The smell was quite breathtaking. It was reminiscent of fish, but imagine the fishiest smell you can, and then multiply it by ten. Now you are getting close to how it smelt. But the really strange thing is that, after five minutes, the smell seemed to disappear. I think that our noses simply became anaesthetised to it, and we stopped smelling it – thank goodness!

Far out to sea a number of fishing boats were busy hauling in their morning catch and through the binoculars we saw any number of gannets plunging in to the water near to the boats, looking just like a shower of white arrows raining down.

"They look so much brighter than the gulls we see around the farm," observed George, sitting down on the cliff edge.

"They're a cleaner white," I responded, "but when you see them close-up you'll be surprised at their other colours; sandy-yellow around the head and bluish-grey eyes that seem to glare at you."

George told me that he'd never seen a gannet before our trip, but he also admitted that there were many other, more common birds, I'd shown him that had previously escaped his attention.

"They are all there, every day, George," I informed him. "Why do you think we don't notice them?"

"Sometimes I think we're just too busy," was his simple, but telling, reply.

"That's an excellent way to put it," I praised his answer. "We're leading our lives at an unnecessarily fast pace. This is an age when there are more labour-saving devices than ever before in the history of the world, and yet we have less time," I said, wistfully.

We both sat in silence for several minutes, lost in our thoughts.

A low growl from Raq brought us back down to earth. The first gannet had returned to its nest.

George gasped as he saw exactly what I had meant about its colouring and marking. A beautiful white body and wings, tipped in black, with a large yet sleek head, crowned in sandy-coloured plumage. Its wide-open eye gave the bird a fierce and piercing gaze. As it was swiftly joined by a heaving mass of other birds, a constant, very loud, 'grog-grog-grog' sound filled the air. The noise became so strong that normal conversation became difficult and we found ourselves raising our voices to be heard.

I pointed to one bird that was almost close enough to touch. Indicating to George that I intended to photograph it, he slowly slid my camera haversack towards me. I gave him a 'thumbs-up' sign by way of thanks.

Gannet

Preparing the camera, I decided that the tripod wouldn't be necessary. I could rest the camera on the ground and get just as good a shot, and it would be nice and steady.

I loaded a plate, focussed on the bird, and its surrounding neighbours, and when I judged its position to be right I pressed the shutter cable.

All the time George was anxiously looking at me. I knew instinctively that he was fired with the success of his owl photograph and would want to take a picture of the gannets. So, unloading the exposed plate and replacing it with a fresh one, I pushed the camera towards him.

"Go ahead," I yelled. "You know how to focus; just wait until the bird's in the right position."

I could see by the way he wriggled about, that he couldn't get a good view. He obviously wanted to photograph a different bird from me, as he began to move more and more to the right and towards the cliff edge.

He got to a place where he seemed satisfied that he'd found what he was looking for. He squinted through the back of the camera, but pulled a face, which said, 'It's not quite right.'

Continuing to look through the camera, he inched further forward, almost like a cat would when it stalks its prey. He was clearly now happy with what he saw, as I watched a look of concentration appear on his face. His thumb pressed the shutter release, and then, suddenly and completely without warning, the edge of the cliff crumbled away, and, giving a stifled yelp, George disappeared out of sight.

Fearing the absolute worst, as the cliff must have been at least sixty feet high, I got to my feet and gingerly stepped towards the precipice. Meg was already peering anxiously downwards. I followed her line of sight, and to my great relief I saw George approximately five feet below lying on a narrow ledge.

"George," I called.

"I'm sorry, Romany," was the response. "The edge gave way. Is the camera OK?"

"Don't worry about that," I said, concerned. "Let's get you back on firm ground."

I had to work quickly. While I felt I could climb down to the ledge, I would then have no obvious means of getting us both back on to the cliff top.

Then an idea dawned. Luckily, in my camera case I had a piece of rope that I sometimes used to secure the camera tripod on windy days. I quickly seized it from the bag, leaned over the edge, and passed the rope to the young lad.

"Grab the rope with both hands, George," I instructed. Beneath us, the sea was crashing against the base of the cliffs. I tried to make my voice and my attitude appear confident, but it occurred to me that we had only one chance at this; any hesitation on either George's, or my part, and disaster would follow.

He was clearly nervous, and I tried not to show my true feelings.

"I'll count to three," I called. "You grab the rope, and I'll haul you up. If you can use your feet to climb, it will make it easier for me to take your weight." I added, "Don't worry; we'll soon have you safe."

I hoped that my voice inspired him.

"One, two …. THREE," I shouted, at the top of my voice. In alarm, many of the gannets flew from their nests, left, right and centre, all the time calling, "grog-grog-grog."

I don't know why, but at that very moment I thought, 'No matter what happens, those birds will still call, 'grog-grog-grog,' long after we are gone.'

George made a grab for the rope. Only one hand made it, the other slipping off. This overbalanced him and caused him to twist to one side. My heart leapt.

He managed to right himself by pulling on the rope, which caused me to lurch forward, but I held on.

George scrabbled around and then his left hand made contact, his fingers struggling to get a good grip.

As soon as I could feel his full weight on the rope I shouted, "Use your feet now," and began to heave.

I leaned backwards, using my body weight to bring George up. The more I leaned back, the less I could see. How much further to go? Could he hang on? Would the cliff edge stand the strain? My mind was in turmoil, so worried was I that he might not make it.

Then, gradually, I began to see his head appear above the edge.

"Keep going!" I shouted by way of encouragement.

Raq and Meg began to bark excitedly. They, too, were feeling the tension of the moment.

Without any encouragement, Meg grabbed the loose end of the rope in her teeth and added her tugs to the process of bringing George safely back on firm ground.

Inch-by-inch his body came clear above the cliff. Then, unexpectedly, his feet reached solid ground and he ran forward a few paces and threw himself down.

Without hesitation Meg dashed to him and licked his face, not giving him time to catch his breath.

The more he struggled to break free the more she licked.

Finally, sitting up, he said, "Meg, I love you, too!"

To me he observed, "Well, that was a close call."

"George, you are the master of understatement," I smiled, adding, "I'm glad you're safe, though."

"Where's the camera?" he enquired.

Glancing towards the cliff edge I saw that it was still there.

"Looks alright to me," I replied.

"Thank goodness," was his answer. "That was a great picture!"

Gathering up the camera, haversack and our other items of equipment, I remarked, "I know we haven't yet had lunch, but I'd be much happier if we were away from this place before we ate."

George nodded his agreement, so we packed up and headed back inland.

Somewhere on the way back to the vardo, facing a walk of at least five hours, George asked a question.

"Romany, can I ask you something?"

"Fire away."

I expected he would want to know something really difficult about life and death situations; maybe he would ask how I might have given his parents the bad news about his accident; perhaps he would be anxious to learn how I might feel if he were seriously injured.

Instead, he asked, "Do you think Meg was worried about me?"

Taken aback, I replied, "You saw how she licked your face? What do you think?"

"Maybe I just taste nice!" he laughed, but I could see the pleasure in his face.

George's Photograph of the Gannet (with a little help from Romany!)

Chapter 10

A hard lesson in balance

"Just look at the height of this grass," I said to George.

"What's this flower – it smells really nice?" he enquired.

"That's meadowsweet," I informed him. "In Elizabethan times it was known as a 'strewing herb.'"

"Whatever's that?" he asked.

"Well," I began, "you have to imagine a time when there were no disinfectants; no shops where you could buy things to clean your house. How do you think your house might smell?"

"Terrible!" was the rapid reply.

"Exactly! What you needed was a strong-smelling flower to hide the smells. And that's where meadowsweet came in handy. Scatter a handful on your floor, walk across it, and your house now smells nice. That's what a strewing herb does for you."

George was silent for a time, which was very unusual, and then asked, "What's that fizzing sound?"

"Fizzing; what do you mean?"

"It's a bit like a saw, only not as loud," was the best he could do.

"I think you mean a grasshopper," I smiled.

"What would you think if I could only talk with my hands and listen with my feet, George?"

"I don't follow you, Romany," he said, with a raised eyebrow.

"That's exactly the way grasshoppers communicate. The fizzing sound is them rubbing their wings against their back legs; it's how they speak to each other."

"I'll stick with talking, thanks," was the simple reply.

Comma was ahead of us in the field. I gave a low whistle; she raised her head, and then slowly made her way towards us.

"She's getting lazy," I observed. "We'll need to be moving on in a few weeks."

George looked dismayed.

"You'll be the first to know when the time comes," I reassured him.

"I'm not sure how I'll feel when Meg goes," George muttered, looking swiftly away.

"And me?" I said.

"Oh, I'll be really sorry, too, when you go, Romany," he said, trying to recover the situation.

Poor George, he had become so attached to Meg. I felt really guilty that I would have to take her away.

By now Comma had reached the fence where we were waiting. I gave her a mint from my pocket and her crunching sounded far louder than it needed to for such a small sweet.

George stroked her muzzle.

"Her nose feels so soft, like velvet," he commented.

Comma bent down and rubbed her nose against Raq.

"They're best friends, you know. They've known each other for at least five years."

Raq's tail wagged furiously. Meg, though, was a little more reserved. Although her tail, too, was wagging, she held back and didn't venture near.

We left Comma and headed off down the slope. Below us ran a long hedge line, made of mixed types of bush, and obviously quite old. The field it bordered was overgrown, yet natural. Long grasses hid who knew what wildlife?

"I don't think I've been here before," remarked George, "even though it's still our land."

Just in front of the hedge I could see the grass moving in an odd way.

"Look over there," I instructed, "just to the left of that dandelion patch. Do you notice anything unusual?"

George strained his eyes to see what I meant. I could see he didn't want to be beaten, but, try as he might, he couldn't identify what was happening.

"Watch the long grass," I told him. "See the way the breeze is blowing it all one way? Now look at the area by the dandelions; it's moving the wrong way, in fact it's twitching. That means there's something there; something we can't see yet."

"I would never have noticed, Romany."

George appeared to be upset with himself for not being able to see what I had seen.

"It takes years of practice to become so observant," I assured him. "I first began watching wildlife when I was about your age. I spent many happy holidays in Cheshire perfecting my skills. We'll make a naturalist of you, yet!"

I gave the dogs a command to stay where they were. Although they weren't happy about it, they did as they were told.

George and I crept forward, stopping every few yards to watch and listen. But whatever was moving around in the grass was oblivious to our presence.

We were within ten yards of the spot, when a large brown rat appeared. George gave a shudder.

"I hate rats. Dad say's they carry disease, and they eat the grain in our barn."

"That's why your Dad likes the owls, of course."

Without warning, a thin brown animal shot into view.

"Weasel," I hissed. "Now the rat's for it."

Spotting the rat, the weasel jumped at it and took it by the throat. The two animals rolled over and over, but the weasel had the better of it.

George turned away. "Much as I hate rats, that was horrible; I'm sticking to watching birds!" He paused, and, almost as an afterthought, he asked, "Do you think we should have done something to stop it?"

"It's the way of nature," George. "Have you heard the saying, 'nature; red in tooth and claw?'"

He nodded.

"That's exactly what it means. One species preys on another to survive. In turn, the rat will have taken other, smaller mammals as its own food. It's called a 'food chain.'" After that brief explanation, I went on to ask him, "So what do you think now? Should we have interfered?"

"I see what you mean, Romany. I don't think we should. What can happen if you do interfere, though?"

"Well, in my experience, every time man interferes with nature, things go wrong as the balance becomes upset. For instance, do you know the story of the rabbits in Australia?" He shook his head, so I went on. "Many years ago there were no rabbits at all in Australia, and then someone decided to introduce a few. Now they are at plague proportions. So much so, that there are plans for a mass removal of them."

George had an example of his own. "What about the grey squirrel, over here?" he asked. "When they were brought here from America they began to take over from the reds. Now it's hard to find red squirrels at all. We don't see any on our land."

"You understand perfectly, George." I continued, "You said earlier that you'd rather stick to bird watching? Well, I'm sorry to say that even in the bird world, the same apparent cruelty happens. Ever heard of a sparrowhawk?"

"Of course; we get them over the farm all the time."

"Where do you think it got its name, then?"

"You mean it takes little sparrows? That's the cruellest thing I ever heard."

"Not just sparrows; many other small birds, too. But again, it's nature's way. It maintains a balance among the species. Sometimes it works to our benefit. Just think; if we had no frogs and toads, we'd be overrun with slugs. If we had no herons, we'd be unable to move for frogs and toads. Each one depends upon the success of the other. Imagine all the flies and midges if we had no swifts."

"I see what you mean," he said, reluctantly. "I'm happy about flies and slugs, but not the things I like."

"That's the problem, George. We can't pick and choose I'm afraid. Just because we think something's attractive, doesn't mean it won't fall victim to some other species."

"I can see the point, Romany," mused George, "but I still wish that it would happen only to the animals and insects I don't like."

I realised that our discussion could go round and round in circles so decided to call it a day!

Chapter 11

The sound and smells of the countryside

Both dogs lay on the grass, panting. We had climbed the steep hillside that ran across the back of Cragg Farm and had sat down to rest, although we had said it was 'to admire the view!'

"That field looks as though it's on fire from up here," George remarked, rather breathlessly. He pointed down to a cornfield that was simply bursting with blood-red, field poppies.

"That's becoming a rare sight as more and more farmers' are spraying their crops to kill what they see as weeds," I observed rather unhappily.

"Dad says that he'll never use these fancy new sprays; doesn't trust them," George told me.

"Well I'm glad to hear it," I said thankfully. "We just don't know the long-term damage they may cause, and they're so unnatural."

"Take a look at the view," I went on. "It's so green and yet we've had such a lot of sunshine. I'd expect the land to be parched dry."

"I imagine the very heavy rain that made you move your vardo has helped," George answered enthusiastically. "Round here we'd had a lot of rain before that downpour, too."

"I'm sure you're right, George. Do you know, I can see the vardo roof from here; to the left, just beyond the haystack," I observed, changing the subject.

George strained his eyes and then gave a smile, indicating recognition.

"There's the farmhouse chimney, too." Now he was warming to the idea! "I didn't realise you could see the farm from here."

Far below us we could see somebody cutting the hay. He was sitting on a machine, which was being pulled by a horse. The faint sound of the cutter drifted upwards through the still air, reminding me of a sewing machine, although I'm sure it was much louder for the farmer beneath us.

George broke into my thoughts. "Dad says that if this dry weather stays with us, we'll have all the fields cut by month end. Last year we had to keep turning the cut hay, to try to get it to dry out," he complained. "Hay that's been damp doesn't get such a good price as in dry years and we have to pay for the workers' wages to turn it every few days."

I marvelled at his knowledge of both farming and business and answered him by saying, "So this dry spell is good news for your Dad and other farmers." Then, hesitating a little, I added, "It will be at the end of the month that I have to move on," breaking the news that I had been dreading to give him.

"Oh, no!" was all George said.

I could see he was looking downcast, so tried to lighten the mood a little.

"I really love the scent of freshly mown hay. What's your favourite smell?"

"Not sure," was the sullen response.

"How about a crop of beans, then?"

"Haven't smelled any."

"Freshly baked bread?" My theory was that speaking of food would rouse some interest, and, sure enough, it worked!

"Oh, yes; especially on a wet morning." His old enthusiasm had returned with the thought of food.

Now that I had his full attention, I posed a question. "Have you ever wondered how important smells are in the animal world?"

"Well, I know that some dogs can find people who are buried in the snow, just by following their smell."

"They're the St Bernard dogs, George. Their handlers train them especially for the task. Every dog has a much better sense of smell that a human, but over the years some breeders have developed the sense more fully in their animals. Most of the dogs we use for hunting - cocker spaniels like Raq, for example - fall into that category."

George thought for a moment. "Would a fox have a very sensitive nose?"

"Most definitely. How do you think Mr Fox finds your chickens at night?" I could see I had his interest, so I continued with a question. "Your Dad farms sheep, doesn't he?" I asked.

"Of course – we've got five hundred."

"So what happens when a ewe gives birth and either rejects her lambs, or if she dies?"

"Dad takes the youngsters to another ewe whose lambs have died."

"What does he do next?"

"He takes the fleece of the dead lamb and wraps it around the other one."

"And why does he do that?"

"You're asking more questions than I do, Romany," he giggled, adding, "I can see where this is leading. It's to fool the mother into thinking that the stranger-lamb is her own baby, from the smell of the fleece."

"See how important smell is in the animal kingdom? You've answered your own original question!"

I paused, and then went back to the rather sensitive point from earlier on. "You know George, although I have to move on, I will be back at some time. You can see Meg then."

"I know you will, Romany, but it's not the same."

"Then we'll have to make the most of the few weeks we have left. Come on, let's make a move."

We headed towards an old and disused quarry. As we neared it, a bird called from some distance away.

"I hear that bird all the time around the farm, but I don't know its name," George stated.

"That happens to be my favourite bird, and it's onomatopoeic, you know."

George looked startled. "Ono- what?"

"Onomatopoeic, George. A big word that's used to describe a creature that makes a sound like its own name, or rather, it is named after its call. Can you think of any birds that say their own name when they call?"

He gave it some brief thought and answered, "Cuckoo!"

"Well done! Any others?"

"I can't think of any," was his short reply.

"How about the chiff-chaff, as another example?"

"I never thought of that one."

We stood quietly for a moment, while we listened to the bird give three, or four more calls.

"So, what exactly do you think it's saying?" I challenged him.

"It's a strange sound; almost as if it's saying that it's feeling 'poorly.'"

"You know that's pretty close. Sometimes the bird books' describe the call as 'coorli.' The bird is actually known as a curlew. When we finally see it, you'll notice it has a long, downward-curving beak. Remember we spoke of how the oystercatcher digs deep in the mud for shellfish?" George nodded his remembrance. "The curlew does the same in its search for food."

Curious, as always, George asked, "Why is it your favourite, Romany?"

"It has two calls, George. The one you've already heard, and the other is a kind of bubbling sound. The first one is very lonesome and mournful and it puts me in mind of open, lonely moorland, very like this land surrounding your farm. The other call reminds me of a mountain stream, just bubbling out of the hillside. In both cases they speak to me of 'wilderness.'"

Raq and Meg were running ahead of us, which caused George to laugh, "I don't think the dogs are interested in the call of the curlew, Romany."

We pressed on, and then suddenly I hissed, "Stop!"

"You gave me a fright, Romany," George whispered. "What is it; is it the curlew?"

"Look; on that large flat rock over there."

About thirty yards away from us sat a delicate bird with grey feathers, a black patch on its head, and a startlingly white rump.

"Do you know what it is?" I asked George.

"Yes. It's a wheatear."

Wheatear

"You never cease to amaze me," I told him. "You're right. However did you know its name?"

He answered, "Every spring it arrives on the farm and I see it flashing its white bottom at me. When Mr Thorpe, my teacher, asked us all to paint a picture of our favourite bird or animal, I painted the wheatear. He said it was very good and he was able to tell me what it's called."

"If the curlew is my favourite because of its call, why is the wheatear yours?" I was expecting an answer such as, 'it always reminds me of spring,' but got an honest, if unexpected, response.

"It helped me to win a bar of chocolate in the painting competition!"

Just then, we heard the curlew's bubbling call that I'd referred to.

"It's exactly as you said, Romany. Just like a stream. I hope we get to see it."

"I think there's every chance," I said, hopefully, "so long as we keep Raq and Meg to heel." I called the dogs and, dutifully, they ran back to us.

"Good girl," George praised Meg in a low voice.

"And what about Raq?" I whispered.

"Oh, he's pretty good too!"

On our hands and knees, with the dogs sneaking along behind us, we crept slowly up to the top of a slight rise in the ground. Peering over the hill, we could see a large bird, grey-brown in colour.

George gave a sharp intake of breath. "Look at the ways its beak curves downward," he gasped, repeating what I'd told him just a few minutes before.

I eased the binoculars from my haversack and passed them to him. He gazed in silence for a minute, or two, then the bird called, "Coorli, coorli, coorli."

From somewhere in the distance, and out of our sight, it was answered faintly by another bird. "Coorli," it said.

"I fully agree with you now," he breathed.

"Do you, George?" I asked. "Precisely with what, do you agree?"

"The curlew is the most onomatopoeic bird I know!"

Chapter 12

Night time in the woods

During the walk back from the quarry, George, as usual, had asked many questions. On this occasion he was particularly interested in the creatures that appear mainly at night. So enthusiastic was he that I promised, providing his parents agreed, we could spend the night in the wood adjacent to the vardo.

I could have guessed that he would go home, check with his parents, and be back like a shot. He did, and he was!

In his excitement all his words rolled together. "Dadsay'sit'sOKwithhimaslongasI'mnotintheway," he blurted out.

"Steady, George; you'll need to slow down a bit," I laughed. His excitement was infectious and the dogs danced around him.

"I can come along, providing I'm not in the way."

"That makes a lot more sense. I suggest we have a good sleep tonight, and we'll spend tomorrow night out of doors, if the weather's alright."

He smiled and nodded.

"Pop over some time after supper, then," I suggested.

The following evening George arrived just as I was putting away my supper dishes. The dogs were already fed, so, gathering up a few things, I began to walk towards the vardo door.

"Aren't you forgetting something?" enquired George.

"I don't think so. What did you have in mind?"

"Something you never leave without," he smiled.

"Ah! My binoculars. Ordinarily I'd take them, but they're almost useless in the dark, so they're just an extra weight, with no real purpose."

"I've still got a lot to learn about watching wildlife," he replied ruefully.

"But you are making a great apprentice!" I reassured him.

We left the vardo behind as dusk was falling.

"You'll be surprised how much darker it will be when we get inside the wood," I informed George.

"I don't think I've ever been out all night," bubbled George, excited to be involved in our little adventure.

Entering the trees, there was a stillness that hadn't been evident at the woodland edge.

"A bit like going into a church," was how George later described the experience.

"This will be a good spot," I said, sitting down. "Use the tree-trunk to support your back; it will be a long night," I warned.

We settled down and I asked George to describe what he could see and hear.

"Not very much," came the short reply.

"Then you're not really seeing and hearing," I countered. "Just wait for a moment, and then tell me what you can hear."

A minute passed, and then he said, "I can hear a kind of whispering, fluttering sound; like somebody muttering very softly."

"Good. What do you think it might be?"

"Somebody watching us?" he said, sounding afraid.

"No, George. There's no-one here. It's the breeze rustling the leaves. What else can you hear?"

"One of our sheep bleating …… and a faint squeaking sound."

"Yes, I heard the sheep. If I'm not mistaken, that squeak is a shrew. They're very short-lived, you know, so they live life at a rapid pace, only sleeping in quick bursts and then off again to find food."

"Why don't we see lots of dead shrews, then?"

"Good question, George. Have you heard of a sexton beetle?" He shook his head. "The sexton beetle," I went on, "is either all black, or black with orange markings. That one is known as the banded sexton beetle. It's not seen very often because it has a very unsavoury lifestyle. It flies to find dead animals and birds and buries them!"

"How?" asked George in a quizzical tone.

"It digs underneath them, and goes around and around, digging deeper all the time, until the body is finally buried; just like the church sexton that digs graves."

"But why does it bury them?"

"This is the most unsavoury bit. The female lays her eggs on the carcase, and when they hatch into larvae, they have a ready store of food to eat."

"You don't mean ...." His question tailed-off as I nodded.

"Have you heard any birds?" I quickly recovered the situation with a new topic.

"Not yet."

"That's because they mostly work on the day-shift; there's a time-gap and then the night-shift takes over."

"What do you mean by the night-shift?"

"Things like bats, owls, badgers and foxes."

"How on earth does something like a bat fly around in the dark with all these trees in the way?" he asked, puzzled.

"There are two things it does. Firstly, it generally flies above the trees, because that's where it will find most insects, secondly it has a sort of echo-locating system. It makes a series of rapid sounds, mainly out of our hearing range, and instantly reads the echo that returns. If there's something in its way, the echo comes back quicker than if nothing was there. You have to imagine that all this takes place faster than you can blink."

"Unbelievable," was all that he could muster in reply.

After a few moments he asked, "Why don't we move around to see what we can find, then?" anxious not to miss anything.

"Well, at night, sound carries much further than during the day. Of course it's much easier to step on a twig and make a sound because you can't see it. I find it works better if you sit and wait for things to come to you. And another thing; whispering is not as effective as talking in a low tone. The higher-pitched sound of a whisper is actually more easily heard than a low, normal voice."

He took the hint and was silent for a while. Suddenly, almost directly above us, there was a 'hoot,' causing us both to jump.

"It's one of our barn owls," he said.

"Tawny owl, George; barn owl's don't hoot."

"I didn't hear it fly in," he said.

"No, because its feathers are specially designed to minimise noise. If it made a sound when it flew, it would find it extremely difficult to catch any prey."

"Isn't nature wonderful?" he sighed and lapsed into thought.

After some time I could tell by his breathing that he'd fallen asleep. The owl had moved on, but it continued to call from afar, otherwise things went quiet for an hour or more, and then I heard a rustling in the grass, some distance away. I nudged George, who awoke with a start. I pointed in the direction of the sound.

"Something quite big," I hinted.

"Fox?" he asked.

"Could be – let's see."

It came closer, and although I strained my eyes, I could see nothing. I could sense George's tension mounting. Then, just a few yards off, by a large tree, a badger came into view. It stopped in its tracks and sniffed the air. The breeze, even though not strong, was blowing from our direction towards the animal which grunted, turned away, and disappeared.

"Wow!" he cried, forgetting the need for silence, but immediately put his finger to his lips, as he remembered. In a soft voice he said, "It was a badger, but I couldn't see it too well."

"Our eyes don't respond as well in the dark," I said. "The best way is to look slightly to one side of what it is we want to see. We have what are known as 'cones' in the centre of the eye, which handle our colour vision and help us see fine detail; 'rods' are packed around the outer part of the eye, and they work best in low light. Next time something comes along, try it out."

We didn't have too long to wait before we both heard a loud snuffling noise approaching us. I knew instantly what it was, but gave George a brain teaser. "That's a really loud noise for a relatively small animal. It's not as small as a mouse, but about one third of the size of an average cat – oh, and you'd need gloves to pick it up."

"Not a rat, I hope?"

I shook my head.

"Squirrel?"

"Not even close – you'll need to hurry, though; it will be here in a moment."

"I'm sorry, Romany, I can't think."

"It's a hedgehog. I saw one when I first came to this area."

It came bumbling along until we could just make it out moving in front of us. The moon and stars were certainly a big help in lighting the scene for us. The noise it made was incredible for such a small creature, and seemed totally out of proportion. George remarked about this and I reminded him of the wren, one of our smallest birds with one of the loudest voices.

Time was moving on and from the direction of the coast, which was to our east, the first hint of light began to show. With that, there was a faint trembling amongst the leaves. "That's often a sign that dawn is about to break. Listen to what happens next."

Within moments, a blackbird began its song. It is usually the first bird to sing in an English wood. Then, as if to remind us of my earlier comment, a wren burst into song, quickly answered by another. Suddenly, the whole wood was alive with birdsong; chaffinches, wrens, blackbirds, great tits, all vying with each other.

"When dawn breaks, why do they all sing like that?" asked my young friend.

"They're staking-out their territory. Each male wants all the other rival males to know that he is singing from his piece of property, and they shouldn't come near."

Then there was an unusual song, hard to describe, but a kind of 'trilling, warbling,' song.

"Any idea what that is?" I asked George.

"Never heard it before in my life."

"It's a wood warbler," I informed him. "The best description I've heard of its song is that it's like a coin spinning on a slab of stone."

"Perfect," he said.

We sat for a while longer as the sun rose and warmed our cold bones. Finally I said, "Come along, then. The dogs will be wanting their breakfast."

"Me too," George answered, so we wandered back to the vardo, where the dogs' show of affection gave the impression that we'd been away for a month. George told me that he'd enjoyed the experience of being outside at night, so I suggested we do it again, but next time close to the farm buildings where we would probably see some different creatures.

We ate a hearty breakfast and George made his way back to the farm.

Chapter 13

Stability

A few days went by, during which I busied myself tidying up the campsite, fishing and writing a few notes in my notebook. These notes are important as they form the basis for my books.

One morning, George arrived at the vardo, heralded as usual by the barking of the two dogs.

Meg jumped up at him in an attempt to lick his face.

"Oy! I've had a wash, thank you," he laughed.

"What are you up to today," I enquired after we had exchanged 'good mornings.'

"Nowt in particular," he responded. "But I was wondering if you'd mind another night outside, as you promised?"

"Of course, George, but you must ask your mother or father first."

"Already have," he grinned.

"The weather looks set to hold," I told him, "so why not tonight? I think this time we'll position ourselves in the farmyard in time to watch the night shift come on duty."

"Another night shift?" he said.

"Of course; it's not only woodland creatures that are out in force at night-time. Be in the yard at 9.30."

He dashed off with an obvious spring in his step. I hoped the night would live up to his expectations.

Just after 9.15 I secured the caravan, leaving the dogs dozing on the floor.

"See you both later," I whispered.

The dusk was beginning to fall as I entered the yard, the scene of our recent owl escapade. From out of the gloom of the barn entrance George stepped, well-wrapped against the potentially cold vigil we were to share.

"What do you think we might see, Romany?" was his opening question.

"I'm not going to say, George; let's just allow things to take their course."

We sat with our backs to the barn wall, the heat of the day still stored in the ancient stones making it a very comfortable place to be.

"Now, George, not too many questions," I warned him. "We need to stay fairly quiet."

He nodded his agreement and our wait began.

Only a few minutes had passed when I became aware of a black shadow fluttering about overhead. I hadn't seen from where it had appeared, although I suspected that it had flown out of the barn. I pointed upwards, put my mouth close to his ear and said softly, "Bat."

He took a second or two to spot it, but then focussed on its ever-moving form.

"Like a piece of rag," he said, remembering to keep his voice low.

Suddenly, a small stream of bats exited the owl-hole above our heads. Whilst it was difficult to count them, I estimated that there were at least ten of them, all fluttering as though they were suspended on elastic.

"You can set your watch by them," I told him. "Providing the weather is alright, they leave their perches within a few minutes of the same time every evening."

"Is there more than one sort of bat?" he asked.

"There are several in Britain, but the most common is the pipistrelle; that's what I reckon we have here. They're also the smallest, about the length of your little finger."

"But they look so much bigger in flight," he commented.

"It's the body size I meant. Their wings make them appear larger, and the fact that they're constantly on the move."

I could see George was rubbing his face and I, too, was troubled by small biting insects.

"I know the midges are a nuisance, George," I sympathised, "but imagine how much worse things would be if we had no bats."

"Why? Do they eat them?"

"Of course; and moths. All night-flying insects are potential prey. Each of them eats many hundreds in a night's work."

We sat in silence, fascinated by the turning and weaving of the winged creatures. After a while, George whispered, "I can hear a faint squeaking sound; can you?"

I had to say that I couldn't. No matter how I strained, nothing reached my ears.

"I think you can hear the bats, George; children often can. As we grow older our ears can lose some of their sensitivity, and that's probably why I can't pick up anything."

"Where do you think they live?" he asked.

"Almost certainly they're roosting in the barn."

"But we didn't see them when we were photographing the owls."

"They're sometimes described as 'mice with wings'," I told him. "They squeeze into the tiniest of spaces, making them very difficult to see. Often the only way to find them is look out for their droppings on the floor. Their roost site will be directly above."

"I'm going to take a look tomorrow," he said excitedly.

"By all means look for the droppings, George, but not the bats themselves. They are very easily disturbed and they won't return to the roost once that's happened."

I knew I could trust him not to alarm them, as his interest in wild creatures was growing by the day. The last thing he would want would be to put any creature off its nest or roost site.

We continued to watch the bats and even in the rapidly fading light we could see them continuing their merry dance, all the while feasting on the thousands, if not millions, of tiny insects that buzzed around the farm.

At midnight, a sleepy George said, "Well, Romany, I knew very little about bats before tonight. I've seen them around lots of times, but always taken them for granted. They'll never be my favourite animals, but I'm grateful for the work they do clearing up so many midges!"

As he stood up to go inside the farmhouse, I told him, "That's a powerful lesson, George. There are many thousands of species of animals, birds and insects in this world. We may never know them all, and we certainly won't love them all, but we must have respect for them all. Every single thing on this planet has its rightful place and nature has set them in balance. Only man has the power to interfere with this natural stability and when he does, it usually spells disaster. If more people would only learn what you have tonight, this world would be a better place for us all."

Deep in thought, George slowly made his way across the yard towards the farmhouse door.

As he opened the door, a quiet, "Goodnight Romany," drifted through the still air.

"Goodnight George," I said.

The Caravan today

Chapter 14

The quarry

As I washed my breakfast dishes one morning, I was greeted with a "Come quickly, Romany," from an out-of-breath George, who had clearly run quite a distance.

I asked him what it was, when the barking of the dogs had died down, and he had recovered sufficiently to be able to speak clearly.

"There's a strange bird-call from the old quarry, and I don't know what it is."

We had visited the quarry on one of our earlier adventures, and although we had seen and heard a curlew, which George had not previously recognised, he was sure it wasn't the 'coorli' call of that bird.

"We'd better investigate," I told him.

Calling the dogs, we headed across the fields and were soon in the base of the quarry. It had obviously been a very busy workplace in the past; evidence of industry was all around. Half-trimmed stones that must have been damaged in the cutting process were scattered about. Some of them showed long, rounded slots, which I took to be the holes that had been drilled out to allow dynamite to be packed inside during the blasting that removed them from their home high above on the hillside.

Above, I could hear the piping call of some meadow pipits, but George said that it wasn't the call he had heard. I asked him to describe it, which, of course, is always difficult.

"It was a bit like 'kee-kee-kee'," he said after some head-scratching.

"Well, I can't be sure from that description," I told him, "but it seems that it might be some sort of bird of prey. I think we'll either have to hear it or see it to be sure. Let's sit on that large rock and wait."

The dogs wandered around for a while and then

settled down in the shade of an overhanging bush. The bees droned in the background and the sound, combined with the heat of the sun, caused my head to nod a little.

Suddenly, I was wide awake. The sound that George had tried to describe was overhead. I lifted my binoculars and scanned the heavens. The blinding sun prevented a clear view, but I was aware of a greyish bird speeding across the face of the quarry.

"If I'm not mistaken, that's a peregrine," I told my young companion.

"Is that a bird of prey, then?" was his response.

"It is, and one of our rarer ones, too," I said. "Let's wait until the sun goes out of sight behind the rim of the quarry. Once that happens we'll have a much better chance of seeing what it is."

Forty minutes passed without another sighting, but by now the conditions were just right. The sun had been replaced by light shadow, making spotting easier.

"Kee, kee, kee," came from a ledge above us and slightly to our right. Focussing my binoculars on the spot, I saw a bird, grey on its back and wings, with dark bars on its otherwise white chest and a distinctive black 'mask,' making it seem a bit like an old-fashioned outlaw!

"I was right; it's a peregrine, George; the black-masked hunter of the skies. Here, take a look," I said, handing him the binoculars.

"Wow," was all he could say. Then followed the usual barrage of

Peregrine

questions.

"Where does it live, Romany?"

"On cliff ledges, just like here."

"What does it eat?"

"Mainly pigeons, but often thrushes and blackbirds."

"Not rabbits, then?"

"Only birds."

"Do the male and female stay together forever?"

"They do during the summer but tend to live separate lives during the winter."

The questioning went on and on, but I was happy to tell him everything I knew.

We spoke about the nest, in which between two and four eggs are laid, usually between March and June, depending on the weather. It is located on a flat ledge and is quite rough-and-ready.

I went on, "Judging by its behaviour, I wouldn't be at all surprised if it has a nest nearby and it's just waiting for an opportunity to catch food."

No sooner had I spoken, than the bird left its high perch and soared across our heads.

"Look," said an excited George, "it's after a pigeon."

It was indeed chasing a bird and gaining on it all the time. Suddenly it climbed above the pigeon, causing George to say, "Oh! He's decided to leave it."

"I don't think so; watch," I replied.

Once it had risen twenty or thirty feet above, it folded its wings into its sides and dropped like a stone. Just before reaching the helpless pigeon, it stretched out its large feet and crashed straight into it. Feathers flew everywhere, and pigeon dangled, lifeless from the peregrine's talons.

"Gosh! That happened so quickly," gasped a stunned George. "I thought it had given up."

"It needs that height to give it that final burst of speed. Let's see where it goes, now. It might lead us to its nest."

Sure enough, as it neared the quarry face, another, unseen bird called, "kee, kee, kee."

"That's the female," I muttered. "He's bringing the food to her, so that means there's a nest. There will probably be chicks there by this time of year, too."

"Can we climb up and look, Romany?" George enquired.

"No, I'm sorry," I told him. "They're far too rare for us to risk disturbing them. We'll have to settle for watching them from here."

We spent the rest of the afternoon watching and waiting, but caught only one more sighting of the peregrine as he flew out of the quarry. I suspected he was sleeping somewhere away from the nest, while the female brooded the chicks.

Over the next week we visited the quarry two or three times, on each occasion seeing one or other of the adult birds busily catching food for themselves or the youngsters. On one memorable occasion we saw the male fly down from the nest site to the river, where he proceeded to wash himself. George remarked that he knew just how cold the river was, because he'd once fallen in. However, I explained how important it was for any bird to have clean feathers. Part of the drying process includes preening; running each feather through its beak and re-distributing the oil that keeps them waterproof. Even in winter a bird needs to bathe, despite the cold.

I had told George that we might expect to see the young birds leave the nest any time, so it was with some disturbing news that he knocked on the vardo door early one morning.

"There are some workmen in the quarry," he said. "I asked them what they were doing, and they said that the quarry had been bought and is being re-opened. Whatever will happen to the peregrines?" he said, anxiously.

"Let's get over there right away," I said.

We hurried across the fields with the dogs running between and ahead of us.

There were five men close to where we had sat and watched the birds on that first day. They were deep in discussion, so I waited a moment, before introducing myself.

"My name is Romany, and I hear that you may be about to start quarrying again," I opened.

"Are you the 'Romany' who writes about nature?" one man asked.

"Yes, that's me," I told him.

"My children love your books and your programme on the radio," he said.

"Thank you very much," I replied, "but if we're right, and you do start quarrying, I'm afraid you're going to disturb some rare birds."

I went on to explain about peregrines and why they were so scarce.

The leader of the group introduced himself. "I'm in charge of this operation, Mr Romany, and I have every sympathy for the birds, but we can't stand in the way of progress, can we? In any case, this is now private land, since the sale, and officially you are trespassing. I shall have to ask you both to leave, please."

His tone became sharper as he finished this little speech, and Raq gave his warning growl.

I called him away and we walked sadly from the area.

"What can we do, Romany?" George asked.

"Not much, I'm afraid. It's their land, and we don't have any authority."

I was shocked at what George said next.

"Well I won't have it. Those birds are rare and have young chicks on the nest. Pigeons are a pest. They eat our corn and we need more, not less peregrines."

I didn't know how to respond, so we trudged back to the farm in silence, where I left him and made my way, with the dogs, back to the vardo.

The very next morning the sound of many voices talking excitedly caused me to look out from the back window of the vardo. Approaching the camp site I could see close to seventy people, adults and children, all talking at once.

I went to the top of the vardo steps and greeted them as they arrived. Out of the crowd stepped George.

"Hello, Romany," he said. "We're here to make a difference."

"Whatever do you mean?" I asked.

"We are all going over to the quarry to protest against the peregrines being disturbed."

Just then, Farmer Swalwell, George's father, appeared from within the group.

"Will you join us, Romany?" he asked.

"Of course I will. Just give me a moment."

I went back inside the vardo to get my binoculars and was soon amongst the band of people, all of whom were determined to save the peregrines.

On the way to the quarry, George explained how he had spent almost the entire evening rounding-up the support of his schoolmates, and how his father had done much the same with his farming friends. Each had his, or her, own reason for wanting to help, but collectively it was the desire to protect something that was worth saving for generations to come.

We reached the quarry-base, just at the same time as a lorry pulled up carrying the same group of men we had seen previously.

The foremen leapt from the cab. "What's this? Don't you know this property is now private?"

Then he saw and recognised me.

"It's you, Romany. I told you to keep off this property."

Before I could reply, George, in a very calm voice, said, "And we told you about the peregrines' nest, sir."

"That's as maybe, but if you don't clear off this land in two minutes flat, I'm fetching the police," he answered, angrily.

"That won't be necessary," responded George. "I've already called them!"

Sure enough, as the discussion continued, a police car arrived, and out stepped two officers in uniform, accompanied by a man in plain clothes.

The third man walked over to George.

"Hello, George; good to see you again, my young friend."

"Romany, this is Mr Spencer, from The Whitby Gazette," George said.

"Hello, Mr Spencer," I said. "What are you doing here?"

"George got in touch last night. He told me about the peregrines and the plans the new owners have for the quarry. He also told me about the protest group that would be coming here. I contacted the police, who told me George had already been in touch, and they offered me a lift. This is going to make a great story for our newspaper."

On hearing this, the Foreman walked over to us.

"Now then, there's no need for all this fuss. The business I represent is always willing to discuss things in an open and friendly way."

"Only since the press arrived!" piped-up George.

"Hear, hear," shouted the crowd.

"What exactly is it you're after?" he asked me, looking rather red in the face.

"Well, as I've already told you, there is a very rare bird nesting here; one that is very important to the local community, as you can see from the people represented here. Farmers want them to be protected because they catch pigeons, which would otherwise destroy their crops. Children want them to be left alone because they understand just how rare they are, and they still want them to be around when they grow up and farm the land for themselves. I want to preserve them simply because they are a beautiful and natural part of this lovely land of ours. Once they are gone, they are gone forever, and I just can't allow that to happen."

All the while, the reporter was making notes in his little notebook, and muttering, "Great. Great."

"I'm sure we can come to some arrangement," the Foremen said, by now looking rather sheepish. "Would it help if we left the quarrying until later in the year, Romany?"

"Of course it would. October, or later would be perfect. The chicks will have long fledged and moved on. However, you would have to stop before March, so that they have somewhere to nest again next season."

"Oh, we couldn't agree to that. Once we start, we'll have to carry on."

"That will look good in The Whitby Gazette!" George said. "The headline will read, 'The company that cares for one season only.'"

"Now, now, young lad," the Foreman said, "let's not get too hasty. I reckon we can manage by starting back up at that time of year; we can always spend the spring and summer breaking the rocks we've blasted out during the winter."

On hearing this, the entire crowd gave a great cheer, and as if by way of a salute, the male peregrine flew overhead, making his, "kee, kee, kee," call.

The reporter continued making notes and interviewing George, his father, and other members of the group, while I spoke to the policemen and thanked them for coming over. They were glad there had been no trouble and were just there to see fair play. They praised George for his intelligence in informing them in advance.

The crowd began to disperse back to their various homes, all feeling good in the knowledge that they had made a real difference.

George, his father and I, walked across the fields. I could see that George was rightly bursting with pride at what he had achieved.

"Today's events demonstrate the power that a small, but determined group of people can have. All it needs is a catalyst; something, or someone to pull it all together, and that was you, George. Well done!"

His father said, "You know, Romany, before today, I thought all this time George was spending with you was a waste. I imagined a boy should be playing football or cricket, or working on his Dad's farm. Now I know I was wrong. I'm right proud of you, George," he said, and I'm sure I saw a tear flicker in the corner of his eye.

George simply blushed, and said, "Thanks Dad."

At the farm, George's parting words were, "I can't see you for a few days, Romany. I've got some work I need to do for Dad."

"I'm sure I'll see you when I call for milk, though," I called, as I walked off down the path to the vardo.

Chapter 15

There's more than one type of caravan

Several weeks had passed at the farm since the excitement at the quarry, and life had proceeded at a leisurely pace.

I hadn't seen George, but I knew he had been busy helping his father with the haymaking; his mother had told me so on one of my daily visits for milk. Since he was last at the vardo I'd put up my old army bell-tent. Although I really enjoy sleeping in the vardo, it is rather small. I'm over six-feet tall and the tent gives me so much more space to stretch out. Also, in very hot weather, just as we'd recently had, the tent is much cooler. I can leave the door-flap open to the stars and allow the gentle night-breeze to flow inside.

I'd spent the day fulfilling a promise I'd made myself when I first arrived in the area. I'd been back to Carr End Farm to photograph the grey wagtail I'd seen on my second day, when I went down to the river for water.

Grey Wagtail

Once I'd found the bird again, I followed it along the river to its nest site, where I set up my portable hide on the nearby river bank.

Over a period of several hours, despite the cramped conditions in the hide, I'd managed to get several really good shots of the bird standing on a nearby rock, pirouetting and bobbing like a tiny ballet dancer clad in a grey and yellow outfit. All that was needed was for me to develop the glass plates in the vardo. Evening is the best time for this as I don't then need to spend a long time blacking-out the windows. So, while I waited for the long shadows to begin to fall, I busied myself cooking supper and feeding the dogs.

Time passed and I judged that the time was drawing close when it would be safe to remove the photographic plates from their protective bag.

Inside the vardo I gathered together everything I needed; the trays to hold the chemicals, the chemicals themselves, and the paper on which to print the photographs. I checked that the dogs were safe inside, and could not open the outer-door to let in the light, and away I went.

I printed three lovely pictures and was about to hang them to dry, when I felt a sharp, stabbing pain in my stomach; I almost fell over, so severe was it. I was finding it difficult to breathe. I had an idea what was happening, as for many years I had suffered with duodenal ulcers, and this felt exactly like the problem I had experienced before. If I could only lie down for a little while, I was sure things would be fine.

I staggered towards the door of the vardo, but felt my legs buckle beneath me. I crashed to the floor, startling the dogs, which ran and hid beneath the bench seats.

My last recollection was of beginning to crawl to the seats as I knew I could not make it down the steps and to the tent. My idea was to rest for a few minutes on the cushions, but it seems I never reached my goal. The next thing I knew was that Raq was anxiously licking my face; I must have fainted.

I found the pain had eased slightly, which encouraged me to make a second attempt. I raised myself on my elbows, managing to get myself into a crawling position. Then, painfully, and very, very slowly, I approached the nearest seat. Using both arms, I levered myself into a semi-standing position and heaved my pain-wracked body on to the cushions.

The exertion of the last few minutes had caused me to break out in a great, cold sweat, and to make matters worse, it had brought back the pain. I collapsed upon the bench, completely exhausted.

Over the next few hours, I lapsed in and out of consciousness. I was vaguely aware of one or other of the dogs checking me over from time to time, but I was powerless to do anything, held as I was, in the vice-like grip of the pain.

By the time dawn had broken, and my position had still not improved, I began to consider ideas for getting help. The only practical option seemed to be that I crawl towards the farm, which opened two possibilities. One was that perhaps I would encounter someone working in the fields; the second was that I would make the entire distance to the farm and obtain help there. Of course, there was a third and very serious outcome, which I deliberately avoided even contemplating.

In order to increase my chance of meeting a farmworker on the way, I decided to put off my epic journey for another hour or two. This delay would also allow me to build the mental strength I needed for the effort.

Time passed, and when I judged that it was approximately nine o'clock, I summoned-up the will to move. Gingerly, I eased myself off the bench; so far, so good. I thought it might temp fate to try to walk, so I crawled to the door. When I saw the steps, I realised how difficult it would be to crawl down them, so turned around and carefully manoeuvred my way backwards, one painful step at a time.

When I reached the bottom, I was already in extreme pain, and exhausted. How would I cover the distance to the farm, if that was what was needed?

I rested for a while and then prepared myself for the long struggle. Carefully, thinking just one movement ahead, I began my journey.

The track leading to the farm was rough and stony, and very soon my knees were cut and bleeding, and my trousers torn through. The dogs ran up and down, thinking it was some kind of game, but this was deadly serious, and I was acutely aware that this trip to the farm could be my last.

Suddenly, the pain in my stomach worsened, and I blacked-out.

Again, I came-to with Raq licking my face. I managed to say, "How will I ever make it to the farm?" to nobody in particular.

Somewhere in my half-waking, half-unconscious state, the word, 'Romany,' kept drifting in and out of my mind, but I was determined to ignore it. I was back in my boyhood, when I spent most of my holidays in Delamere Forest, in Cheshire. I was sitting on a fallen tree at the side of Cholmondeley Mere, a large lake on the Cholmondeley Castle estate. In the clear water, I could see fish swimming about. Tomorrow I would return with my fishing-rod, to try my luck.

"Romany," (a pause), "Romany – are you alright?" The voice became loud, and insistent.

"Romany; please wake up. It's me, George."

I opened my eyes, and sure enough, George was by my side, peering concernedly at my figure lying prostrate on the ground.

"George; I need help; quickly. Can you fetch a doctor?" I pleaded.

"I don't like to leave you, Romany," George said, tearfully.

"I'll be OK. Go now, please."

He ran off in the direction of the farm, giving many backward, anxious glances. I quickly lapsed back into unconsciousness, and this time, in my mind, at least, I was cycling from my boyhood home in Liverpool, to my holiday home in Cheshire. My bicycle would be called a 'boneshaker' by today's standards, and yet I was happy to be free of school, where the teachers and pupils referred to me as 'black-eyes;' a reference to my dark, gypsy appearance. I always stayed at Oak Tree Farm, near Bickerton, where, each year, the Ruscoe family welcomed me into their home. Many were the adventures I had in the fields and lanes, leaving the farm early in the morning and returning last thing at night.

In my dream I was about to climb a tree near to Oak Tree Farm, when I was again brought back to reality by, "Romany; I'm back."

Upon opening my eyes I saw that there was not only George, but a number of people standing over me. Only one I recognised; George's brother, Wilf. The other two men wore a uniform, which identified them as ambulance-men. So, it had come to that!

After some preliminary questions, and a gentle examination, I heard the two men talking to George and Wilf. The phrase, 'have to move him,' was all I could make out.

All four came over to me and one of the men explained, "You'll need to go to hospital, Romany, but we've got to get you to the ambulance first. It's parked at the farm, which is the closest we can get to you. It means we'll have to carry you there on a stretcher."

I nodded, feeling I was in good hands.

The stretcher was brought close to where I lay, it was unfolded, and a blanket laid over it. Then, very carefully, and under instructions from the man who had spoken to me, I was lifted, slowly and carefully on to the stretcher. The pain made me wince. The ambulance-man must have spotted this, for he said, kindly, "Soon have you safe, Romany."

He gave an instruction and all four lifted the stretcher. Then, taking their time to ensure that I wasn't bumped, we made our way up the long slope to the farm.

Considering the distance, and my weight, the boys did so well in getting me safely to the ambulance, which was in the farmyard.

Grannie was waiting for us as we arrived. She came over and wished me well, adding, "Get back to us soon, Romany," to which I smiled weakly.

After a count of four, they lifted me aboard the waiting vehicle.

As I entered the door, I wanted to say something nice, especially to George for finding me, but the first thing that came to mind was, "Oh well, George, out of one kind of caravan into another!"

George on horse with brother Wilf at Cragg Farm

Chapter 16

Moving on

I was taken to Whitby Cottage Hospital, where I found I had been correct; I had indeed been suffering from duodenal ulcers. The doctor kept me under sedation for three days, by which time my condition had improved.

Concerned for the welfare of Raq, Meg and Comma, I enquired of the Matron whether she had any news about them.

"Oh, that young boy who has been in every day is looking after them."

"That will be George," I thought.

"The news of you being in here has spread far and wide," she told me. "We've had so many people telephoning and popping in to see how you are. I hadn't realised you were so famous."

"That's the power of radio for you," I answered.

Later that morning, another boy called in to see me. With him, he had a bunch of sweet peas for me. His name was Peter Burton.

We chatted for a while about the countryside, the birds he had seen and my radio programmes.

"I'd love to go 'Out with Romany,'" he said, quoting the title of my programme.

"Well, why don't you come to the vardo when I'm better? I'll give you directions."

We agreed that I would drop him a line when I was coming out of hospital and make arrangements for him to visit.

Later in the afternoon, George came along to wish me well. He told me that the dogs were coping very well at the farm and that Comma was fine in the fields. We chatted about birds he had seen since I was last on the farm, and I could see he was doing his best to cheer me up.

When the time came for him to go, I explained that I would need some time to recover, and that the hospital had suggested I might go to a cottage right on the seafront at Sandsend. Because it was quite a long way from Cragg Farm, he might have difficulty in getting there to visit me. He told me that nothing would stop him, which I really appreciated.

When I was well enough, I was moved to the cottage by the sea. Whilst it was small, it didn't matter, as I wasn't allowed from my bed. Although I found it difficult to be tied to one room, the compensation was that I was able to look out to sea from my bedroom window; in fact, all I had to do was to prop myself up on my pillows, and I had a wonderful view of the ocean.

One day, as I was gazing longingly from the window, I saw a little girl wander into view; I guessed she would be about eight to ten year's of age. Every so often, she would stop and peer down into one of the many rock-pools along the beach.

After she had looked at four, or five, she went to walk on, but suddenly went back to the last pool she had inspected; it was obvious she had something that really excited her, as she was almost jumping on the spot!

She carefully knelt at the edge of the pool and slowly dipped her hands into the water. She waited patiently for what seemed like an hour, but, in reality, was probably only a few minutes. I so wished I could walk over to see what was so interesting. Then, in an instant, she pulled her hands from the water, and out onto the sand flopped a large fish! So that was it! The fish must have become trapped, not noticing the receding tide. It had been waiting for the arrival of the next tide to swim out to sea, but no such luck.

I watched her pick up the fish and head towards the steps in the sea wall, very close to where the cottage was situated. She disappeared from view as she neared the wall, but reappeared a moment later, having reached the top of the steps. I took my chance and called her from the window. She came over, and I complimented her on her good work. Rightly proud of what she had done, she showed me the fish; it was a sea trout, sometimes called a salmon trout.

She asked if I was Romany of the BBC, which I confirmed; news obviously got around that part of the world! We talked a little longer and I learned that her name was June; I felt rather pleased when she told me that she felt she knew me well, just before she went on her way.

The time passed so slowly in my little cottage, even though the owners were very good to me, providing everything I needed, especially rest. However, with a little patience, the time came for me to leave.

Saying goodbye to the elderly couple was difficult, especially after all they had done, but I was itching to be back at the vardo.

Farmer Swalwell had arranged for a car to collect me and it was on the drive back that I decided it was time to move on. I had friends on a farm in Cumberland who, hearing of my illness, had asked me to spend some time with them. I was looking forward to taking the vardo back on the road for the long trip to the Eden

Valley. What I did not relish, though, was the thought of telling George that Meg and he were to be parted.

We arrived at the farm and I thanked the driver for collecting me. Almost the second I stepped from the door, Raq, Meg and George came out to greet me. The noise made by the dogs' barking was almost deafening and I couldn't understand what George was saying. When they finally calmed down, he said simply, "It's good to have you back, Romany, but I expect you'll be wanting to move on."

This took me totally by surprise and all I could do was nod, weakly.

He made things very easy for me, by adding, "I've been expecting this, Romany, so Meg and I have already said 'good-bye.'"

I had a lump in my throat when I replied, "George; that's so brave of you. Well done."

We headed to the vardo and when I opened the door I was greeted by the old familiar smell; a friendly and welcoming mixture of lamp-oil and wood smoke.

George asked when I was leaving and I told him that it would be the day after tomorrow. I had promised Peter Burton that he could drop by before I went and had arranged that for the next day. However, I told George that I would call at the farm as I left, to see him and to thank his father for his hospitality.

He departed and I watched him trudge across the fields, head bowed, clearly unhappy.

The following morning Peter popped by. We spent a pleasant time talking about his interest in wildlife. I thanked him for coming to see me when I was in hospital and, with his Box Brownie camera, he took a few photographs of the vardo, one or two including Raq and me. In fact, I've included one at the beginning of this book. Meg seemed a little shy with Peter, and didn't want to get too close, so was left out.

After he had gone, I busied myself around the vardo, making sure all the moveable objects were safely stowed away for tomorrow's trip. I then went to check Comma.

As soon as I called her, she ran to me and I gave her an apple, which she crunched with relish. "Back to hard work in the morning," I told her, while I scratched behind her ear. She whinnied as if to say, "I know and I can't wait!"

We had an early night so as to be ready to face the morning. And so, for the first time in over three weeks, I spent a night in the vardo. I lay in bed for a while thinking about my time in the area. Many things I had planned to do, I had achieved. I was looking for a change of scenery and to see some different birds and animals. I'd also made some new friends. True, I had no idea I would end up in hospital, but then does any of us know what the future holds?

I slept soundly and was awake with the dawn chorus. I never realised how much I had missed the song of the birds when I was hospitalised.

After we had all had some breakfast and the final dishes were away, I fetched Comma and harnessed her to the shafts. Because of the steepness of the slope, I decided not to ride on the step, but instead I led Comma by the head and we zigzagged upwards across the fields to the gate we had entered all that time ago.

Closing the gate behind me, I took a final look down the slope and decided that we would return some day. Then, hopping on the running board, we were off down the lane.

In just a few minutes we pulled up outside the farmyard gate, right next to the wall where I had first seen George all that time ago.

The squeak of the vardo wheels and the clop of Comma's hooves must have alerted the family, for out of the door poured Mr and Mrs Swalwell, Grannie, Wilf and George.

The farmer broke the silence. "You're away, then?"

"I am, Mr Swalwell. It will take me several days to reach the next farm in Cumberland. There's a young fellow there, who's about George's age; Arthur Kidd's his name. I imagine we'll have some adventures there, too."

I thanked him and the family for all their help and hospitality. Then, turning to George, I said, "And to you, young man; we've had some great times together. I hope you don't forget the dogs and me in a hurry."

"I promise I won't, Romany," he whispered, sadly.

I climbed back on the vardo, calling to the dogs, which obediently jumped up beside me. A flick of the reins and the vardo lurched into movement, quickly settling into its familiar, swaying rhythm.

I looked back and saw the family waving; all except George, who was sobbing uncontrollably. I glanced at Meg, whose head was hanging down, her ears flat against the side of her little head. She was also a picture of unhappiness.

As my old vardo reached a bend in the lane, I said, "Meg; go to George."

Without needing any further instruction, she leapt from the running-board and ran back to the farm. "She's yours, George," I shouted, and the farm was lost from sight behind the trees.

The Author

Phil Shelley was born in Liverpool in the early 1950's. He developed an interest in wildlife after moving North of the city in his formative years. Birdwatching remains a passion, although he is also an avid guitarist and singer.

He works as a business consultant and specialises in improving the interface between people and processes.

Romany's life, works and environmental ideals have become something of an obsession with Phil and he enjoyed immensely the opportunity to produce a story about his hero that is part fact, part fiction, but always true to the spirit of Romany.

The Artist

Ray Leonard Hollands obOSB MRICS MFPWS MASI MRSH, was born in 1942 and studied art initially at the Heston and Isleworth Evening Institute whilst also an architectural trainee, and then, on a one to one basis, under Bertram Armitage, son of Alfred Armitage, minor artist of the Newlyn School.

He is first and foremost a Wildlife Artist, his special interest, as a life-long ornithologist, being bird paintings in which he endeavours to create an "alive" image (some of them have been used as cards for the RSPB of which he is a Life Fellow), but, taking his inspiration from the marvels of Creation, Ray also paints abstracts and landscapes. Ray's work, therefore, is varied and of wide appeal. He works mainly in oil and acrylic and sometimes in gouache.

More of his work can be seen at **www.dorsetvisualarts.org** and **www.britanniaarts.co.uk**. In each case enter Hollands in the search box.

Printed in the United Kingdom by
Lightning Source UK Ltd., Milton Keynes
140524UK00002B/214/P